Pr...
Ludmilla ...

"This celebrated Russian author is so disquieting that long after Solzhenitsyn had been published in the Soviet Union, her fiction was banned—even though nothing about it screams 'political' or 'dissident' or anything else. It just screams."
—*Elle*

"Her suspenseful writing calls to mind the creepiness of Poe and the psychological acuity (and sly irony) of Chekhov."
—*More*

"The fact that Ludmilla Petrushevskaya is Russia's premier writer of fiction today proves that the literary tradition that produced Dostoyevsky, Gogol, and Babel is alive and well."
—Taylor Antrim, *The Daily Beast*

"Her witchy magic foments an unsettling brew of conscience and consequences."
—*The New York Times Book Review*

"What distinguishes the author is her compression of language, her use of detail, and her powerful visual sense."
—*Time Out New York*

"There is no other writer who can blend the absurd and the real in such a scary, amazing, and wonderful way."
—Lara Vapnyar, author of *There Are Jews in My House*

"A master of the Russian short story."
—Olga Grushin, author of *The Dream Life of Sukhanov*

LUDMILLA PETRUSHEVSKAYA was born in 1938 in Moscow, where she still lives. She is the author of more than fifteen volumes of prose, including the *New York Times* bestseller *There Once Lived a Woman Who Tried to Kill Her Neighbor's Baby: Scary Fairy Tales* (2009), which won a World Fantasy Award and was one of *New York* magazine's Ten Best Books of the Year and one of NPR's Five Best Works of Foreign Fiction. Earlier works include the short novel *The Time: Night* (1992), which was short-listed for the Russian Booker Prize, and "Svoi Krug" (1988; "Among Friends"), a modern classic about the late-Soviet intelligentsia. A singular force in modern Russian fiction, she is also a playwright whose work has been staged by leading theater companies all over the world. In 2002 she received Russia's most prestigious prize, the Triumph, for lifetime achievement.

ANNA SUMMERS is the coeditor and cotranslator of Ludmilla Petrushevskaya's *There Once Lived a Woman Who Tried to Kill Her Neighbor's Baby: Scary Fairy Tales* and the literary editor of *The Baffler*. Born and raised in Moscow, she now lives in Cambridge, Massachusetts.

There Once Lived a Girl Who Seduced Her Sister's Husband, and He Hanged Himself

LOVE STORIES

LUDMILLA PETRUSHEVSKAYA

Selected and Translated with an Introduction by
ANNA SUMMERS

PENGUIN BOOKS

...rk 10014, USA
...oronto, Ontario M4P 2Y3,
...oks Ltd, 80 Strand, London
...blin 2, Ireland (a division of
...t, Melbourne, Victoria 3008,
Australia (a division of Pearson Australia Group Pty Ltd) · Penguin Books India Pvt Ltd, 11
Community Centre, Panchsheel Park, New Delhi – 110 017, India · Penguin Group (NZ), 67
Apollo Drive, Rosedale, Auckland 0632, New Zealand (a division of Pearson New Zealand Ltd) ·
Penguin Books, Rosebank Office Park, 181 Jan Smuts Avenue, Parktown North 2193, South
Africa · Penguin China, B7 Jiaming Center, 27 East Third Ring Road North, Chaoyang District,
Beijing 100020, China

Penguin Books Ltd, Registered Offices:
80 Strand, London WC2R ORL, England

First published in Penguin Books 2013

1   3   5   7   9   10   8   6   4   2

"Milgrom" was translated by Anna Summers and Keith Gessen. It first appeared on the
Words Without Borders website.

"Give Her to Me" first appeared in *The Baffler;* "The Goddess Parka" in *Playboy;*
"Hallelujah, Family" in *Zoetrope;* and "The Wild Berries" in *The Paris Review.*

The stories in this collection were published in Russian in *Neva, Octyabr,
Aurora, Znamya, Novyi mir,* and *Literaturnaya gazeta.*

LIBRARY OF CONGRESS CATALOGING IN PUBLICATION DATA

Petrushevskaia, Liudmila.
[Short stories. English. Selections. 2013]
There once lived a girl who seduced her sister's husband, and he hanged himself : love stories /
Ludmilla Petrushevskaya ; selected and translated with an introduction by Anna Summers.
pages ; cm
ISBN 978-0-14-312152-7
1. Petrushevskaia, Liudmila—Translations into English.   I. Summers, Anna, translator.
II. Title.
PG3485.E724A2 2013
891.73'44—dc23   2012029559

Printed in the United States of America
Set in Stempel Garamond   •   Designed by Elke Sigal

This translation is dedicated to my loving husband, John, and to the memory of my mother, Irina Victorovna Malakhova, who taught me to love Petrushevskaya.

Contents

CONTENTS

My Little One

A Happy Ending

Introduction

Loving Petrushevskaya

Russians have a word, *byt*, from *being*, to denote the circumstances of everyday life. In Ludmilla Petrushevskaya's love stories, *byt* means waiting in line for basic goods, from potatoes to winter shoes ("Young Berries"); it means inflation that robs old people of their savings ("A Happy Ending"); it means an ambulance that takes an hour to come to a dying woman ("Two Deities"); it means alcoholism, obsolete ideology, anti-Semitism, poverty, inhumane laws—all the follies and cruelties of late- and post-Soviet society.

Above all, *byt* means a shortage of housing.

After the Russian Revolution, thousands of ruined peasants poured into Moscow. The state outlawed private ownership of housing, and so family apartments across the city were turned into rooms, which then were divided and subdivided until, eventually, there remained corners no larger than the size of one prone body, plus one suitcase. Over time these communal apartments were broken up, and families were moved into cramped, ghoulish blocks of apartments. By 1972, when Petrushevskaya published her first story, the city was ringed by concrete buildings made of one-, two-, and three-room apartments that often housed several generations of Russians. It is in these small, overcrowded, uniform, much-coveted units that Petrushevskaya's love stories take place.

Born in 1938 in Moscow, Ludmilla Petrushevskaya never knew family life. Evacuated with her mother to Kuibyshev during the war, she was left there in the care of her aunt and grandmother while her mother returned to Moscow to attend college. Members of the family of "an enemy of the people," they were treated as pariahs—and were slowly starving. At age eight Petrushevskaya began to run away from her temporary home and spend summers as a street beggar. Her mother returned after four years and brought her back to Moscow, where they were officially homeless. As a young girl there, Petrushevskaya and her mother lived under a desk in her insane grandfather's room, while occasionally renting cots in nearby communal apartments. It was an unsettled, unhappy childhood, one experienced without the consolation of siblings. And it did not exhaust her misfortunes. For her first husband died young, leaving her a widow struggling to support herself, their son, and her mother all together in one small apartment. She didn't meet her father until after college.

These seventeen love stories represent the complete arc of Petrushevskaya's writing life, from her first published story in 1972, "The Story of Clarissa," to "Like Penélope," published in a 2008 collection marking her seventieth birthday. The four sections tell of glimpsed romances in their earliest stages (A Murky Fate); of the twisted and accidental circumstances in which families are thrown together (Hallelujah, Family!); of parents struggling to raise children without murdering each other (My Little One); and of mature romances that have run their course or have been realized in a new form (A Happy Ending).

But the stories collect toward a thematic center in the drama of maternal love—the only kind of love that can survive in extreme spaces, the only kind that *must* survive if families are to endure. In the ironically titled "Hallelujah, Family!" a fourteen-year-old girl seduces her older sister's husband. The husband, discovering his sister-in-law is pregnant by him, hangs himself. What follows is a tale in which motherhood burns off the abrasions of experience, or *byt*, only to acquire fresh ones. The girl who seduced her older sister's husband gives birth to a daughter, and that daughter gives birth to her own daughter. Her mother (the daughter of the girl who seduced her older sister's husband) loses her mind from the burden of her family's history and from the fact that her young daughter, now sleeping with older men, gives birth (without a husband) to a daughter, the fourth generation in the story.

Many of these stories portray the redemptive potential of maternal love displaced onto damaged men. In "Ali-Baba," a childless, abused woman meets an apparently healthy man, a fellow alcoholic, in a bar, and goes with him to his apartment—and to an unwelcome surprise. "Eros's Way" portrays a prematurely aged woman who has lost her femininity to the hardships of *byt*, who comes to life when an insane, married man appeals to her maternal instinct. The same story shows a successful mother doing herself in, adamant for her child's undivided affection while poisonously suspicious of ingratitude and betrayal. "A Happy Ending" shows a betrayed wife reconciling with her husband only after he has grown as helpless as a child.

But these are not tidy tales of loss and redemption. The love that her characters are feeling is like dreaming, a passion too complex and mysterious to be named, much less resolved. As with dream interpretation, which thrives in densely settled societies and represents a longing for personal freedom, love's interpretation in tiny Russian apartments is stacked with too many layers of ambiguity and ambivalence ever to produce a wholly known emotional world.

Petrushevskaya's genius as a literary artist lies in her ability to make the strangeness of her mothers, her would-be mothers, her once-were mothers, and her other characters worthy of our sympathy in the partial absence of our understanding. The changes she introduces in vocabulary, perspective, rhythm, and intonation sneak up on us, and before we know it we have implicitly forgiven bizarre, bewildering, and often vulgar behaviors and qualities. "Tamara's Baby" begins with an exposé of a homeless, deranged man who travels to a sanatorium, one of the modest country resorts where urban Russians flocked for a romantic fling, a portion of serendipity, or a private escapade unthinkable back in their cramped apartments. The deranged man encounters a kindly older woman who takes his arm and, surprisingly, takes him in. The woman's motives for sheltering the stranger are so perverse they cannot be called romantic. Nor does the resolution allow a conventionally sappy reading of two deranged persons united by their common alienation from society. No, the man and the woman can barely understand each other. Petrushevskaya evokes their quiet gratification nonetheless, and leads us to the epiphany hinted at in the story's title.

"A Murky Fate," meanwhile, gives us an aging, unmarried, and childless woman who invites into her overcrowded apartment a fat, balding, married coworker for a few undignified moments of sex. Why? The next day, she inspects her feelings and discovers that she cannot live without him, and this discovery, instead of breaking her heart—instead of condemning her to the pain and humiliation of unrequited love—makes her weep with happiness. At first we feel a mix of disdain and exasperation for the pathetic heroine, but by the end we are weeping with her, for her. She believes she has found a semblance of love. Who are we to deny her?

Petrushevskaya worked as a journalist in radio, television, and trade magazines, but it was as a playwright that she first made her name. Theater companies embraced her dramas, which expressed her miraculous ear for the registers of colloquial speech, from the self-serious, educated speech of the intelligentsia to the hilarity of sputtering alcoholics. As in her plays, so in her stories: Petrushevskaya listened on crowded subway platforms, on playgrounds, in apartments, and in other locales of ordinary life. All the stories in this collection have happened. All these sad and strange characters have real counterparts.

And so Petrushevskaya's stories had to be suppressed; editors distrusted her pessimism, while official critics accused her of blackening reality. It was not until 1988, when she was fifty, that her first book of prose was permitted to circulate. Her stories contained no scenes of bloody repression, no labor camps, no knocks on the door in the black night—no politics at all. What appeared to be domestic stories of fringe characters, however, conveyed a verdict as brutal as the most overt dissident fiction. In place of the heroic new men and new women, Petrushevskaya offered a cast of pathetic characters barely holding themselves together. Her continual flow of insight into the emotional psychology of late- and post-Soviet society, her collective portrait of imperiled humanity that's always been the highest object of communist idealism, must have terrified cultural bureaucrats in charge of official reality. For in her love stories, the revolution, having begun with the promise of communal apartments, degenerated and died in those same apartments. The juxtaposition of the fate of her characters and their high expectations for love and respect was unforgiving—and unforgivable.

I grew up in one of the concrete apartment buildings that have surrounded Moscow since the seventies, in the care of a mother who adored Petrushevskaya's fatalism as lived reality and taught me to read her in the same spirit. When her stories first circulated, the shock of recognition was terrible indeed among my parents' generation. Petrushevskaya, it turned out, had been writing about their lives; it was their claustrophobic apartments that she described, their ungrateful children, their sick parents, their frustrated marriages.

In college during the hopeful nineties I returned to reading her, and what struck me then was the atypicality of her stories. In Russia's culture the kind of stories shared with strangers on crowded buses and subways are extreme, the stuff of urban legends, myths, and folklore. Later still, when I became a wife and mother, I learned to read her with a smile, to delight in her humor, her irony, her steadfast refusal to save her characters, or her readers, from themselves.

Petrushevskaya waited for many years to see her first book into print, and in spite of official suppression, she never stopped writing. She couldn't have kept her talent and her spirit alive on the diet of self-pity. No, even her gloomiest stories whisper their moments of humor, irony, and, yes, redemption to those readers willing to listen. She wants us to be strong, and clever, and resourceful, like the Russian people she loves.

ANNA SUMMERS

There Once Lived a Girl
Who Seduced
Her Sister's Husband, and
He Hanged Himself

A Murky Fate

A Murky Fate

This is what happened. An unmarried woman in her thirties implored her mother to leave their studio apartment for one night so she could bring home a lover.

This so-called lover bounced between two households, his mother's and his wife's, and he had an overripe daughter of fourteen to consider as well. About his work at the laboratory he constantly fretted but would brag to anyone who listened about the imminent promotion that never materialized. The insatiable appetite he displayed at office parties, where he stuffed himself, was the result of an undiagnosed diabetes that enslaved him to thirst and hunger and lacquered him with pasty skin, thick glasses, and dandruff. A fat, balding man-child of forty-two with a dead-end job and ruined health—this was the treasure our unmarried thirtysomething brought to her apartment for a night of love.

He approached the upcoming tryst matter-of-factly, almost like a business meeting, while she approached it from the black desperation of loneliness. She gave it the appearance of love or at least infatuation: reproaches and tears, pleadings to tell her that he loved her, to which he replied, "Yes, yes, I quite agree." But despite her illusions she knew there was no romance in how they moved from the office to her apartment, picking up cake and wine at his request; how her hands shook when she was unlocking the door, terrified that her mother might have decided to stay.

The woman put water on for tea, poured wine, and cut cake. Her lover, stuffed with cake, flopped himself across the armchair. He checked the time, then unfastened his watch and placed it on a chair. His underwear and body were surprisingly white and clean. He sat down on the edge of the sofa, wiped his feet with his socks, and lay down on the fresh sheets. He did his business; they chatted. He asked

again what she thought of his chances for a promotion and got up to leave. At the door, he turned
back toward the cake and cut himself another large
piece, then licked the knife. He asked her to change a
three-ruble bill but, receiving no reply, pecked her
on the forehead and slammed the door behind him.
She didn't get up. Of course the affair was over for
him. He wasn't coming back—in his childishness he
hadn't understood even that much, skipping off happily, unaware of the catastrophe, taking his three
rubles and his overstuffed belly.

The next day she didn't go to the cafeteria but
ate lunch at her desk. She thought about the coming
evening, when she'd have to face her mother and resume her old life. Suddenly she blurted out to her
officemate: "Well, have you found a man yet?" The
woman blushed miserably: "No, not yet." Her husband had left her, and she'd been living alone with
her shame and humiliation, never inviting any of her
friends to her empty apartment. "How about you?"
she asked. "Yes, I'm seeing someone," the woman
replied. Tears of joy welled up in her eyes.

But she knew she was lost. From now on, she understood, she'd be chained to the pay phone, ringing
her beloved at his mother's, or his wife's. To them
she'd be known as *that woman*—the last in a series
of female voices who had called the same num-

bers, looking for the same thing. She supposed he must have been loved by many women, all of whom he must have asked about his chances for promotion, then dumped. Her beloved was insensitive and crude—everything was clear in his case. There was nothing but pain in store for her, yet she cried with happiness and couldn't stop.

The Fall

That summer we watched a transformation by the sea. We were staying across the street from a resort for workers; she was one of the guests. We couldn't ignore her—she was too vulgar. We overheard her laughter on the beach, at the local wine seller, on the way to the market—everywhere. Just imagine her: a tight perm, plucked eyebrows, gaudy lipstick, a miniskirt, new platforms. It was all cheap and tasteless but with an attempt at fashion. She strained, pathetically, from her curls to her heels, and for what? To look no worse than the others, not to miss her chance—her last one, perhaps—for a little womanly happiness (as imagined in soap operas). A blue-collar Carmen, searching for some seaside romance.

So here's the setting: the sun, the sea, a new perm, and—attention everybody—she's off to the fruit market with a pack of admirers representing every breed. At the head of the pack parades a tall one in a heavy wool suit, despite the heat (we nickname him Number One). He is followed by a potbelly in a shapeless tank top; next comes, incongruously, a skinny youth with hippie locks; and the procession is finished by a runt in a tracksuit—he's obviously there for a drink. Our Carmen laughs shrilly, but not as shrilly or loudly as one would expect—her laugh is not the war cry of some neighborhood whore who invites all and sundry to her table; this Carmen laughs softly. She doesn't want to collect every male in sight—she's already got plenty; any more, and things could get out of hand. The tall one, in the meantime, maintains his position at the head of the pack. He's the hungriest and toughest in her entourage, the alpha male with the most serious intentions.

Seriousness rules the ball—soon, the other suitors vanish, and Carmen and Number One are now seen together. Number One has changed his winter suit for a pair of sober gray shorts, which she must have selected for him here at the resort. Carmen and

Number One walk about with dignity: she's curbed her laughing; he carries her purse. They follow the resort's regimen of eating breakfast at the dining hall, then taking in the sun on the beach, then visiting the produce market for fresh fruit.

On the crowded bus to the market they stand as a single unit, the top of Carmen's head barely reaching Number One's chin, even with her in those atrocious heels. She keeps looking up, not meeting his eye—the sign of a serious crush, by the way. Number One gazes abstractly over everyone's heads, looking out for his little lady—and suddenly anyone can see these two are in love, that they have separated from the crowd. And so the crowd shuns them, spits them out. In this sweaty pell-mell they are marked, singled out, doomed.

Yes, it's happened to them, the biggest misery of all—a doomed love. Both look sad, on the verge of tears.

In the elapsed days Carmen has mellowed and acquired a golden sheen. Her ridiculous curls have loosened up and lightened in the sun. Blond and delicate, no worse than any movie star, she seems lost, consumed by her doomed passion. Number One hasn't changed, only darkened from the sun, like a workhorse in the summer that will lose its color in winter. But he, too, seems marked by the grief that shadows hopeless romance. He seems tense and steely, like someone facing the end point of his fall. What awaits them is worse than death. What awaits them is eternal separation.

Yet there they are, trying to dance, clutching each other to the beat of that summer's pop anthem. Her purse is still bouncing on his arm. A few days remain. At the beach they walk away from the crowd, from cots and umbrellas sunk into the sand, and disappear in the sunlight.

The new season has begun. The beach is crowded with shapeless white bodies and smug new faces. Our golden couple has departed. The delicate Carmen and her faithful husband, Number One, are jetting through the frozen air away from each other, back to their children and spouses, back to the cold, and to hard, grim work.

She'll wait for his long-distance call in a phone booth at the post office. For ten prepaid minutes they'll become one soul again, as they did over the twenty-four prepaid days of their vacation. They'll shout and cry across thousands of miles, deceived by the promise of eternal summer, seduced and abandoned.

The Goddess Parka

A.A., a schoolteacher in a provincial town, decided to spend his summer vacation near a lake and woods, not far from where he lived. He rented a screened porch in a cabin (he couldn't afford a whole cabin) and began to live there very quietly. He left in the morning with a backpack and returned late at night; he never asked for anything and refused offers of dinner leftovers, to the chagrin of his landlady, who had planned to charge him for food or, at least, for the use of a hot plate.

A.A.'s search for privacy and independence didn't take into account a certain Aunt Alevtina, a resident of Moscow and his landlady's distant relative. Alevtina visited the cabin every summer. She'd stay two weeks and leave in a van loaded with fresh preserves. She lived in a small room in the landlady's shed, a room she had equipped with a small television and refrigerator. She paid the electric bill by a separate meter at the end of her stay. Again, the landlady was left without a profit, although, to be fair, her grandkids did stay with Aunt Alevtina in Moscow over Christmas holidays and got to see the Kremlin.

On the night of Alevtina's arrival, the landlady was boiling a samovar on pinecones. She opened the conversation with complaints about her miserly tenant. "Stingy like you wouldn't believe: first thing he tells me is he isn't going to use any power! Unmarried, too."

"Huh?"

"I said *unmarried*. Thirty-five years old. Not a crumb on his porch. What does he eat?"

"Maybe he catches the bus to town, goes to the cafeteria there."

"Ha! The bus doesn't stop here most of the time. . . . Well, so how about my black currant—will you buy any this year?"

"Only if the berries are large."

"Large! After all the work, all the watering . . ."

And the irritated landlady went on to recite the virtues of her black currant, hungry for a deal. Alevtina, rumor had it, lived in Moscow in great comfort and even wealth. At the thought of Alevtina's riches, the landlady wanted to boast; she mentioned two magnificent apartments she'd given to her daughters and their worthless husbands when her old house was demolished. One husband was a policeman, the other a fireman at a factory; he worked one day and slept two, but try to get him to fix the roof and he's too busy watching soap operas. His brats are shipped to Grandma's every summer, and she's expected to provide all the meals, and so forth.

At this moment, A.A. slipped through the gate and climbed onto his porch. He reappeared with two buckets, filled them with water from the well, and began washing himself down to the waist. The two Penelopes watched him over their teacups.

"Alexeich," the landlady called out with dignity, although a bit uncertainly. "I say, help yourself to what fruit's on the ground."

"Excuse me?" The teacher quickly retreated and disappeared.

Alevtina giggled, but the landlady, undaunted by the teacher's clever escape, pressed her point loudly.

"Thirty-five, like I said, and nothing."

"What do you mean, nothing?"

"Well, you know, a waste . . . of goods."

"What goods?" pretended Alevtina. In fact, from the moment the landlady mentioned A.A. she'd been poring over all those women she knew in Moscow who were withering from drudgery and loneliness, while right here was a healthy specimen with four limbs who didn't stammer and was mentally stable (with some luck).

"You don't think he has a lady friend in Komarovka, eh?" Alevtina asked.

"How would I know?" the landlady croaked, and then stood up to go to bed early because, she explained importantly, she was allergic to the sun and got up to pee at four. She relieved herself under the berry bushes, "for fertilizer," and shuffled inside.

Little stars sprinkled across the darkening sky. Alevtina sighed deeply in the direction of the porch. Nina, that's who he needs. Thirty-seven years old, a pharmacist, mother died recently, lives in a studio on the outskirts. Her few admirers had been shooed off by the old witch, who had been correct: where would the newlyweds sleep—under mama's bed? (Nina's mom was a distant relative of Alevtina's husband.) Well, well, hummed Alevtina. She held her breath and waited. The unborn child also waited in the dark. Nothing stirred. Black silhouettes of the apple trees loomed in the twilight. The warm air smelled of phloxes.

A.A.'s shadow cut through the orchard in the direction of the outhouse. Alevtina liked his deftness. A few minutes later A.A. emerged and exhaled the foul air. Alevtina pounced.

"Good evening, sir. How can you explain yourself?"

"Excuse me?" A.A.'s foot froze in midair.

"I don't need your excuses. How much do you owe?"

"Who, me?" A.A. thought for a second that the woman mistook him for someone else, and instead of fleeing to his porch and hiding under the blanket, he took the first step toward the samovar.

"I'm not going to yell at the top of my lungs—there are people sleeping," Alevtina remarked drily.

A.A. approached her gingerly. In the twilight, heavy Alevtina resembled a bust of a Roman emperor. She addressed A.A. imperiously.

"So, how are we going to solve this problem?"

All of a sudden A.A. began to babble something about the well, saying it wasn't his fault the well was empty by the end of the day, he took five gallons and used his own buckets, others took fifty to water their vegetables, and so on.

"I see. Well, we'll find a solution somehow. Remind me your name again?"

"Excuse me?" That was one of A.A.'s favorite evasion techniques, perfected on his pupils.

"It's Andrey, correct?"

"Could be."

"So how about a cup of tea? I have all this hot water left. What do you say, Andrey Alexandrovich?"

"No, thanks. Actually, I'm Andrey Alexeevich. . . ."

It was the height of summer, the blessed time when fruit and berries ripen and fall. Alevtina hired a van and loaded it with jars of preserves. A.A. did all the loading, while the driver, a local resident, watched him idly. (Tormented by rumors about fabulous Moscow wages, local men had stopped working altogether and were swiftly turning into full-time alcoholics.) The landlady, too, watched Alevtina's evacuation without offering to help. But suddenly she jumped: the teacher grabbed two huge canvas bags off his porch, threw them into the van, waved her good-bye, and left with Alevtina! The landlady had been right in the middle of a fantasy in which she got rid of the useless fireman and married her younger daughter to her tenant.

In the van, Alevtina, too, was thinking that A.A. was the husband she'd want for her daughter if only she had one, but instead there was a son and a leech of a daughter-in-law, and an only grandson, the light of her life. The boy was fourteen; he spent most of his time examining his pimples, and he refused to speak to his grandmother even on the phone. For him Alevtina had spent her vacation sweating over the stove, boiling and pickling—the boy loved her cooking. Her own son ate hardly anything—he preferred homemade liqueurs to food—but her daughter-in-law shoveled it in by the pound. (She also smoked and cursed like a plumber, and frequently suggested they discuss "future arrangements" concerning Alevtina's property.)

At the end of this golden summer day, the van wheeled into the beautifully maintained yard in front of Alevtina's building. They loaded all the jars into the elevator and then carried everything into Alevtina's spacious one-bedroom apartment, which was decorated with rugs and a crystal chandelier. On the train back, A.A. fantasized about an apartment just like that, in the same neighborhood, and also a sweet wife, and a boy of his own whom he could teach everything he knew. He'd quit his wretched public school where kids munched on sunflower seeds and wore headphones to class. All this came to pass some years later.

He met Nina at Alevtina's birthday party (Alevtina had wired him money for the train). By that point Alevtina must have broken off with her daughter-in-law, because none of her family showed up. Nina didn't impress A.A. She was heavy, very shy, with large pale eyes. But he did notice her casual, almost indifferent manner when she was examining some old prescriptions of Alevtina's—the manner of a true expert. The next time he saw Nina was at the hospital. He had come to see his dear Alevtina at his own expense, significant for his small salary. Alevtina spoke in a clear voice, though with some effort, and gave him a considerable sum—"for books." She managed not to add "to remember me by." Although A.A. didn't cry, he must have looked pretty miserable, because Nina's eyes filled with such sympathy and kindness that he had to turn away. Only after they were married did he find out that Nina alone had looked after Alevtina, feeding her pureed soups and fresh juices and staying with her every night after work.

It was Nina who sent him the final telegram. His train was late, and A.A. had to run through the subway. He then took the wrong exit and got lost; for directions to the morgue he asked the only person who was out in that terrible neighborhood, a woman with a dog, and she told him precisely—she must have known the place from personal experience. At the morgue he was asking small groups of people where they were burying such and such, but then he saw Nina and throughout the ordeal stood next to her. Everyone else in the party stared at him wildly, but later, at the crematorium, they asked him to help carry the coffin, as if accepting his presence. Nina didn't cry, just trembled. Alevtina looked serene and very young; she had lost a lot of weight. They closed the coffin and hammered down the lid.

The crematorium bus took them back to the city and dropped them off in the middle of an unfamiliar street. Tipsy relatives crowded the sidewalk. Finally one of the cousins announced that close friends and relatives were invited to the wake. He avoided looking at A.A.; they all avoided him. Suddenly a drunk woman, a cousin, pointed at him and inquired loudly, "And who is he? What's he doing here?"

"This one's looking for a drink," explained the grandmother.

Alevtina's fat son, Victor, sidled up to Nina.

"So how are things? Married yet? Come to the

wake, get something to eat, to drink. You should come to all our get-togethers, you know. Where else will you go? And who is he?"

"A friend," Nina said after a pause.

"Right. Look, you'd better make me your heir—you never know what to expect with out-of-towners."

"What do you mean, my heir? Don't I have sisters?" Nina seemed shocked.

"Idiot! If you marry him, he'll inherit your apartment! He can kill you just to get it!"

Here A.A. spoke up in his teacher's voice, "Nina! It's getting late." And Nina simply turned her back on Victor and walked away. She walked slowly, with the put-on dignity of a freshly insulted person. A.A. tore after her: at the very least he had to find out how to get to the subway, and he guessed she was headed there. He was too cowardly to ask his future wife for directions and just trudged behind her. He was leaving for home on a night train.

Suddenly a small truck drove up onto the sidewalk in front of A.A. and began unloading. A.A. wanted to walk around it, but a wave of pedestrians forced him back. By the time he made it to the other side, Nina had disappeared. He didn't know her last name, and there was no one to ask. Alevtina used to speak so much about Nina, about her wretched life with a difficult, ailing mother whom Nina had endured to the end after her two sisters couldn't take it anymore and left the old woman. A.A. used to listen to these stories with an inward smile: he understood perfectly well what was behind them, and he also knew why Alevtina had called for him at the hospital. He'd always resisted Alevtina's scheming—he had been resisting Nina silently for a long time—but now that Nina had disappeared, there was no one to resist, and his life lost its meaning.

Ten hours remained before his train. He stood in front of the subway station in the freezing wind, cold and hungry, aching from unrelieved tears. Then he turned around and walked back to the truck where he had last seen Nina. From there he returned to the subway station. He shuffled back and forth between the truck and the subway, and then he saw her: she was running in his direction, crying, her enormous eyes searching for his. They fell into each other's arms. He scolded her for running off like that—he'd almost lost her! Then he begged her to calm down, to stop crying—everything was fine, they'd found each other—and he took the heavy bag from her unfeeling hand, like all husbands do, and they walked off together.

Like Penélope

There once lived a girl who was beloved by her mother but no one else. The girl was used to it and didn't get too upset. Her name was Oksana—a glamorous, fashionable name—but our heroine wished for something plainer: Tanya or Lena or even Xenia. She was a serious-minded young lady, tall but not very graceful.

Oksana studied forestry in a third-tier college—the only one she could attend for free. Upon graduating she could expect to get a clerical job in a state agency tallying birches and firs on paper. She and her mother shared a two-room apartment in a standard concrete building. In one respect their housing situation stood out: right below them, on the third floor, lived an incredibly noisy family of violent alcoholics. Every night the floor shook with screams, banging, and knocking; the lady of the house regularly interrupted her partying to stumble outside and yell "Murder!" and "Help!" Oksana tip-toed past their ravaged door; outside she dressed in dark clothing and wore her hat low over her face.

This was because she came home late, when it was already dark: she had the precious opportunity to take an affordable evening English class her school had introduced. Her mother told her about a certain Vladimir Lenin, who had learned a new language by translating a page of text into Russian and then back into the language, and Oksana adopted Lenin's method, translating texts about logging, rafting, and skidding—clearly her college expected its students to haul timber on the Thames. The students pro-tested, insisting that England didn't need Russian loggers with college degrees, and begged to be taught normal spoken English.

At that time, Oksana's mother was unemployed. She had set aside her hopes of being hired as an editor and tried to pick up at least some copyedit-ing. She called publishers and received "test assign-ments": a novel in two volumes, an action thriller of five hundred pages, a pharmacology textbook. Two weeks per project. At first Nina Sergeevna laughed at these assignments and their illiterate language and quoted the best lines to Oksana: "a passerby passed by" or "he was sitting on a seat." Driven by professional pride, she stayed up all night rewriting these miserable tomes down to the last comma. But when she tried to reach her so-called employers, she always ended up speaking to their secretaries, who told her that, alas, she hadn't passed the test. Oksana rightly suspected that these so-called publishers took advantage of her mother's free labor. To make ends meet, Nina Sergeevna worked as an attendant at a day care center, where she shared a tiny unheated booth with an overfed mongrel, a kind of guard dog who never left her quilted blanket and responded with nervous barking to the voice of the teacher behind the thin wall.

Soon this existence, already meager and not very happy, changed for the worse. One night there was a long-distance call: it was Klava, the mother of Nina Sergeevna's first husband, who had died very young, calling from Poltava in Ukraine. This Klava visited Nina even after she remarried and had Oksana; she used to bring bags of boys' clothes that had belonged to her grandson, Misha. Before long Klava lost her younger son, too. Misha's mother remarried and moved to Israel, but Misha refused to leave his school and friends and moved in with Klava. For years Oksana had to wear Misha's hand-me-downs, including an emerald tuxedo with padded shoulders that made her cry. Oksana had never met Misha, but she couldn't stand him. And there you have the background to the midnight call.

The former mother-in-law informed Nina Sergeevna in an expressionless, metallic voice that Misha had lost everything; people whom he owed money had taken over his company, and Klava had had to sell her apartment and move into a summer shack. The shack is made of plywood, Klava droned, the water and power are turned off after the summer, and someone has filled her well with trash. The firewood has run out; she tried to burn tree branches, but they wouldn't burn. The cold has been incredible this winter—already it's started snowing. She went to the city to collect her pension but steered clear of her former building: Misha told her she may be taken hostage if someone recognizes her. A happy New Year to you all, Klava concluded her monologue.

Nina Sergeevna used the pause to invite Klava to come stay with them, then hung up the phone and stared with her big eyes at her tall daughter, who stared back. "Here we go again," concluded Oksana with a sigh. She was used to her mother's almost daily acts of irrational charity. The most recent one happened just the day before at the Belorussky Station. Nina Sergeevna was crossing the bridge, sadly contemplating her editorial career that ended in a guard's booth, when in front of her she noticed a tall woman with ramrod-straight posture who walked woodenly and carried a pile of snow on her head like a Pushkin monument. Nina Sergeevna bypassed the strange creature and hurried toward the warm metro station. But the woman caught up with her and asked if she was going to Minsk—because she was; that is, she wanted to, but she had no money— she'd been cheated. She came from Belarus, she said, having brought with her some cosmetics for sale, but the buyer didn't show up, and she wasn't paid. The woman produced a Belarusian passport. Nina Sergeevna told her to come inside the metro station, it was too cold to talk in the street, but the woman looked at her in terror: "Are you going to give me away to the cops?" Ah, of course! The poor thing didn't have a Moscow registration and could be arrested at the entrance to the subway! Nina Sergeevna asked how much she needed to get home. The poor woman tried to calculate: five hundred thousand, no, three hundred thousand, no, three hundred rubles! Nina Sergeevna gave her the money and also a baguette she'd been carrying home. Three hundred rubles was exactly one third of what remained of her pension after paying the rent. Thank God the monument hadn't asked for five hundred or a thousand— Nina Sergeevna would have satisfied any request for help; often she didn't wait for people to ask and just gave away what she had.

Two days later they picked up Baba Klava at the station. Baba Klava had some luggage with her: the familiar backpack with summer work clothes from her dacha, two paper icons, and a sack of apples. Misha the grandson had forbidden her to go back to the apartment, and as a result Klava had not a stitch of winter clothing and was wearing a summer shirt in December.

At Nina Sergeevna's, Klava installed her paper icons behind the glass front of the bookcase. She prayed to them constantly yet, she believed, discreetly. Her apples were left to rot under the kitchen table: Klava expected them to ripen by New Year's Eve. She shared Nina Sergeevna's sofa bed in the walk-through room but couldn't sleep—she did her best to lie still between Nina Sergeevna and the wall. Meanwhile, the tired mother and daughter slept dreamlessly, treasuring every moment of rest.

Nina Sergeevna got back in touch with a half-forgotten friend who dabbled in philanthropy. That friend helped her get an appointment at a decent secondhand store, and Nina brought home a warm jacket and two quilted house robes for Klava, and also a length of light, gold-toned material—a former curtain. Oksana asked her mother sharply what the rag was for—they had plenty of rags as it was. "They offered; I took it," explained Nina Sergeevna innocently. "Looks like silk, almost."

Later, Klava reluctantly recounted the tragic events that had led to her homelessness. Misha the grandson had had a small publishing business that printed calendars. He'd wanted to expand, and so he put out an expensive monograph by a Moscow artist (who had convinced Misha that he was the artist of the moment). The book didn't sell, and Misha owed money all around. The meter was ticking, and finally his creditor sent "shakers"—thugs who shake out money.

By then Oksana was taking classes part-time, in the evenings, and had found work at a landscape design company. Graduation was postponed by two years. She was paid very little but did impeccable work for both the owner and her bookkeeper. What Oksana missed most was her English class. She always carried in her purse the same book, *The Hound of the Baskervilles*, and tried to read it on the train but immediately would doze off.

In her free time Nina Sergeevna worked on getting poor Baba Klava recognized as a Russian citizen or at least a legal resident, so she could see a doctor. Moscow's plutocracy treated Klava as a foreign spy, simply because she was Ukrainian, and denied her all rights. After talking to fellow sufferers in endless lines, Nina decided she needed to go to Poltava to get a piece of paper from the local archive saying Klava had been born in Stavropol and was therefore a Russian citizen. Klava froze up. She was terrified the shakers would find out her address in Moscow. When the exhausted Nina returned with the necessary paper in hand, Klava asked in a fearful whisper whether Nina had visited her house. "Of course not!" Nina told her lightly. "I only stopped by the city hall and came right back. You will now receive your citizenship and a pension!"

When Klava went to watch television, Nina explained to Oksana that she had visited Klava's courtyard and chatted with some neighbors, that was all; told them she was a Muscovite wanting to move to Poltava—were there any apartments for sale in that building? Nothing, they told her. But, she said, apartment ten had just been sold, she'd heard. No comment. When she was leaving, one of the women caught up with her and took her phone number. Oksana almost fainted. "When will you learn to think? Why did you give that woman our number?"

"You know how I can read people!"

"That's right, you read that monument from Belarus the other day real well."

"This woman, Valentina, mentioned Klava: she remembered Misha as well as his mother, who had immigrated, and his dead father, Klava's son. She used to work as a pediatric nurse and treated Misha as a child. I spoke to her, true, but I knew what I was doing!"

"Oh, Mama. I bet we'll have visitors soon." And Oksana was right.

Late at night on December 28, the phone rang out with long-distance calls. "Oksana, get Klava, quick!"

Klava's body formed a little bump under a heavy blanket. The bump was trembling. "Who is it, shakers?"

"No, no, it's Misha's mom calling from Jerusalem!"

As soon as Klava said hello in her metallic voice, the connection broke. "Couldn't bear to speak to me. Finally remembered Misha. Too late—he's probably gone," Klava said, and marched off to the bathroom.

The next day Oksana brought home from her office a small potted juniper—a Christmas tree. "Oh, juniper," Klava whispered solemnly. "Just like the one on our family gravesite. My two sons are there, and my dear husband. Thank you, Oksanochka." Klava's mood was solemn these days. She loved watching TV police dramas in which justice temporarily triumphed. They calmed her down but didn't make her any more optimistic.

Nina Sergeevna was busily working on the piece of almost-silk from the secondhand store. The prerevolutionary Singer filled the little apartment with knocking. Klava was in the kitchen making a holiday pie with the rescued dacha apples. Oksana was trying to study in her little room when Nina Sergeevna emerged with a pile of golden fabric.

"Our New Year's present to you, honey," she tentatively addressed her stern daughter. "To wear when you go out!"

"Mama! Stop imagining things! I'm not going out, and I'm not wearing this!"

"But, honey, Klava worked on it, too! She used to be a professional tailor. Remember the green tuxedo? She made it herself!"

"Tuxedo? Mama! I have finals in two weeks! My boss wouldn't give me any time off! She says she can't afford to give me time off—she's supporting a husband. She yelled at me for an hour. Now think,

Mama: Do you really believe I can be interested in your secondhand garments?"

Klava walked into the room, saw the heap of silk, pursed her lips, and whispered, "Sorry, Oksanochka, I used to sew well, but my hands are not what they used to be. Nina, I told you she wouldn't wear it!" She turned back to the walk-through room and loudly began to pray.

Oksana glanced at the clock: an hour before New Year's. She took a bath, then sat down with wet hair at her old computer. Nina Sergeevna stroked her shoulder. "Please, baby. Klavochka is terribly upset that you won't even try it on. What will it cost you? She is eighty years old!"

From Klava's room came loud mumbling. Oksana gave in. In the bathroom, in front of the little mirror, she changed into the new dress. It was a very open evening gown with a slip and a weightless scarf to cover her bare shoulders. The scarf's edges were embroidered by Nina Sergeevna. For goodness' sake, thought Oksana, why did she waste her time on this embroidery? Who's going to see it? Who's going to see me? Her future of endless toil, without romance or happiness, flashed before her eyes. A messy office with bookkeeper Dina, an aging beauty from the provinces whose daughter refused to speak to her; her boss Olga, an emaciated workhorse with bags under her eyes, darting from client to client in a broken-down car. And the clients, wives of the new Russians, with their dreams of garden gnomes and potted junipers as seen in soap operas and their contempt of simple Russian trees. Suddenly Oksana reached for her never-used cosmetics purse and brushed her lashes thickly with mascara, shook out her damp hair to create a wave, applied her mother's blush to her cheekbones, painted her lips generously. Why she was doing all this, for whom, Oksana didn't know. New Year's Eve. New dress. Black hair down to her waist. Big, rosy mouth.

Oksana stepped into the hall. The usual bangs and screams could be heard from the apartment downstairs. Oksana opened the door to her mother's room. Nina's eyes widened. "Klavochka!" she yelled in the direction of the kitchen. "Come here! Our princess has put on your dress."

Klava pursed her lips into a tight smile and announced, "Like Penélope like Cruz." The Moscow *like* had become Klava's default expression of strong emotion.

Nina Sergeevna laughed with delight. "Once, at the dacha, years ago," she said, "we all decided to go mushroom picking, and our neighbor Vera—she was at least eighty at the time—dashed over to the mirror and started painting her lips. My mother said to her, 'Aunt Vera, we are going to the woods; who's the lipstick for?' And Vera replied—I'll never forget it—'Who knows? Maybe that's where *it* will happen!'"

Klava pursed her lips again, Oksana shrugged, and the doorbell rang. Nina opened the door a crack and saw a strange young man.

"A happy New Year to you, ma'am," said the man. "You should call the cops: somebody's getting killed downstairs."

"Don't worry, the cops stopped coming here a long time ago. They'll come when someone finally dies, they told us," said Oksana's mother, shutting the door and then rushing to the kitchen, where the chicken was burning. The doorbell rang again and kept on ringing. Oksana sighed, grabbed the phone, and shuffled to the door. Alcoholics are human, too, she thought—let them use the damn phone.

The young man was still standing on the doorstep, holding his expensive leather suitcase. When he saw Oksana, his jaw dropped. "Excuse me," he mumbled, "may I speak with you?"

"What is it?" Oksana asked impatiently.

Suddenly Klava began screaming, "Misha!" Downstairs a man drunkenly yelled, "Friend, friend, come back!" and a woman begged them to call an ambulance—their own phone had been disconnected. Klava continued screaming, "Misha, is that you?"

The stranger nodded silently, staring at Oksana, unable to say a word. "May I come in?" he finally asked—the voices from downstairs were approaching. Oksana sighed and stepped aside.

"Babushka, please stop yelling; let me get undressed," said Misha. Then he addressed Oksana: "May I ask your name, Miss?"

Oksana looked at him with her enormous eyes, straightened her long neck, and answered quietly, "Xenia."

"Xenia," repeated Misha. "What a lovely name. I need nothing else in this life."

Klava was brought to the scene. Oohs and aahs, hugs and kisses followed, along with Misha's assurances that Klava would have a new apartment; that everything would be taken care of—here are some presents for everyone.

Mama Nina observed her daughter and wondered where this new slow grace in her movements had come from, the twinkles in her laughing black eyes, the wave in her hair, the gorgeous dress. . . . Of course: she had made it herself.

Ali-Baba

They met in line outside the bar, but that didn't mean anything—people meet in all kinds of places. Ali-Baba glanced over her shoulder, saw his blue eyes and his good suit, and thought, "Aha," without suspecting how easy her prey would be. Victor watched her little dance without interest. He knew no woman of sound mind would pick him up; they could always smell it on him. Five or six years ago he might have worked up some excitement, but now he just waved them away, the pretty ones who made eyes at him. In this case, though, there wasn't much to wave away—just an ordinary-looking Jewish woman with large dark eyes.

Victor's boss had dispatched him to an office near the bar to deliver one thing or another (after a series of mishaps, he'd been demoted to courier). Finding the place empty, he decided to lunch early on liquid bread, as he called beer. The establishment lifted him to the level of respectable people—Ali-Baba, for example—although he wondered briefly what a well-dressed woman was doing among cursing men. The bar was located in a good neighborhood and had some pretense of design (little lights on the walls), but there was the swearing, not to mention the cleaning woman who swiped half-empty pints, pretending they were empty. (Angry customers once stormed her closet and discovered her chasing one down; a scandal followed, but the police didn't get involved.) Since Victor and Ali-Baba were waiting in the same line with the same end in mind, they began talking—a harmless exchange between decent citizens.

They discussed this and that but mainly how long one had to wait here and at other places. Ali-Baba knew all the local spots, including the Saigon, to Victor's growing respect. Ali-Baba was beginning to see that Victor hadn't been spoiled with attention, and she felt a kind of protective tenderness for him, as if he were a stray kitten of a rare breed. Inspired by this warm feeling, she began to recite aloud a long love poem, originally composed for her latest life partner. Recently that partner had tossed her over the railing of his balcony for stealing his booze. She hung four floors above the ground, clutching at the railing, until two truck drivers forced their way into the apartment and rescued her. Her beloved was hiding in the kitchen, inventing a scenario for the police: that *she* had tried to kill *him*. As soon as the ambulance called by the neighbors was gone, the beloved, seized by an unforgiving fury, gathered up her things and tossed them over the same railing. Ali-Baba had managed to crawl down the steps, to pick her stuff up off the pavement, and to reach her mother's apartment. She'd been staying there ever since, still unable to work or even to unbend her fingers. The visit to the bar was supposed to mark a new beginning.

"Another?" Victor asked. But she insisted on buying this round, and again he marveled at her manners and sophistication. Already he had paid for six rounds and had just enough money left for two more pints. This money was to last him until his next paycheck—that is, the whole next week. Ali-Baba didn't mind: she was flush from selling another volume of her mother's edition of Alexander Blok. (Her mother didn't know it, but she now owned only four volumes of Bunin's works out of her original nine.) Ali-Baba told herself that since half of her mother's property was hers, she might as well make use of her half. Her mother was undergoing medical tests at the hospital and didn't know that Ali-Baba had returned to her apartment. Otherwise she would have checked Ali-Baba into rehab, as she had done twice before.

Ali-Baba usually preferred to stay at her friends' apartments. By now she had one girlfriend left, Horse, and recently Horse had found a man, Vanya, who beat her (and her guests) to a pulp. Vanya preferred his own friends, movers from a nearby supermarket, who supplied him with booze and food. As for Ali-Baba's numerous gentlemen friends, they all lived with their wives or mothers, so staying the night was out of the question. That very morning Ali-Baba's mother had called home from the hospital to see if her phone line was working, and Ali-Baba had answered without thinking. The mother called back again and again, but Ali-Baba didn't answer. She gathered up some things—the volume of Blok, her mother's new panty hose and makeup, and a bottle of sleeping pills—and was soon standing in line outside the bar.

To Ali-Baba's delight, Victor wasn't married and lived alone, without his mother. Victor wasn't overjoyed at her request to stay the night but in the end agreed. They got to his house; he unlocked the door to his communal apartment, then the door to his room. It was warm and completely dark and also a little smelly. Victor turned on the desk lamp and changed the sheets, and the two began their night of love. Ali-Baba was pleased to have shelter for the night, and Victor was pleased because he found clean sheets and received a decent woman in style. Overwhelmed by a sweet, almost maternal feeling, Ali-Baba began reciting the same love poem, but before she could finish, Victor fell into a rhythmic snoring. Ali-Baba stopped her recitation and drifted off, too. Almost immediately she woke up: Victor had peed the bed.

Ali-Baba leaped off the filthy sheets and changed into her clothes in the reeking darkness. She perched on a chair by the desk and cried softly. Now she understood why he was alone, why he hadn't protested when his wife left him with a tiny room and took a whole apartment. To the accompaniment of Victor's snoring, Ali-Baba reviewed her life and swallowed the pills. The next morning Victor found her lying facedown on the desk. He read her note and called an ambulance. Paramedics pumped Ali-Baba's stomach, then took her to a mental hospital. Shaking with a hangover, Victor pulled on some clothes and trotted off to work to wait for the liquor store to open.

Ali-Baba was lying in a clean bed in a ward for the insane. She would stay there at least a month. Soon there would be a hot breakfast and a conversation with a friendly doctor. Later, as she knew, her neighbors would swap life stories. Ali-Baba also had a story or two to share. She wanted to tell them, for example, about the first time she took pills, when she went blind for twenty-four hours. The second time put her to sleep for two days, but the sixth time she woke up in the morning fresh as a daisy.

Hallelujah, Family!

Two Deities

In reality, life doesn't stop with a wedding, with he-roic action, or with happy coincidence, as in films, when a certain person misses his boat (*Titanic*) or, as in this case, when an unmarried woman of thirty-five decides to keep the child born of a random tryst with a boy of twenty. They were having a little office party; all five employees were dancing and drinking, including our Evgenia Konstantinovna (Genya), the senior editor in glasses. Young Dima, their courier, looked at his watch with a tragic expression, because he lived far outside the city and the subway had al-ready stopped running for the night. Never mind, he told them, I'll get there somehow (it was a cold November night). Evgenia Konstantinovna and Dima spent that night together.

How did it happen? Upon arriving home, with the uneasy Dima in tow, Genya saw her grandmother's cane in the corner of the hall. Her grandmother had practically raised Genya. Later on, she sold her country house to buy Genya a studio apartment in Moscow. The grandmother, of course, now visited without warning—she had her own set of keys. And if Genya wasn't home, then her grandmother would stay all night waiting for her.

The cane in the corner suggested this might be one of those nights. Very quietly Genya made up a kind of bed for Dima on the narrow kitchen sofa, using a towel and a tablecloth for sheets. She gave him another towel for the shower, then showered herself. When she came out she found Dima curled up on the short sofa like a dollar sign. He was clearly suspecting something—young boys are scared of older women, just like girls are scared of grown men. Poor Genya lowered her head onto the kitchen table and quietly began to cry. She couldn't tell him about the cane—he wouldn't understand. As everyone in the office knew, he lived in the same house as his two beloved grandmothers, not to mention his mother and aunt. All those women must have doted on him ever since he was a baby, and now he began to stroke Genya's hair, gently pulling her toward him. They managed to fit on the tiny sofa. Dima didn't dare undress Genya; he simply hiked up her skirt. The first time was chaotic, the second a little better paced—during army service Dima had acquired theoretical knowledge, which he now applied. The grandmother never left the room.

Early in the morning Dima jumped off the sofa, kissed Genya on the forehead, and ran off to his remedial courses. They never slept together again, but eight and a half months later Genya gave birth to a son.

Why did she keep the baby? When later that morning she finally peered into the room, she didn't find anyone there, just the cane and her grandmother's purse in their usual places. Genya's next-door neighbor told her that, coming home late from the theater, she found the grandmother in the doorway, unconscious. The ambulance didn't come for an hour, but when they finally took her, the grandmother was still alive. The neighbor's voice was full of reproach. Two weeks later, having buried her grandmother, Genya vowed to keep the child who was now her only family—a touching but impractical decision.

Dima soon transferred to another department as

a junior editor; he was preparing to enter college, was overworked, and always greeted Genya with a luminous smile, the way people greet their old teachers whom they'd love to chat with if only they had time. By spring, however, his sunny expression became a mask of stunned politeness, for Genya had grown very big and shuffled around heavily; she still looked relatively well groomed, despite the ungodly heat, only her lips had puffed up like an African woman's, and she constantly wiped them with a big crumpled handkerchief. Dima continued to smile politely at her, appearing not to notice her transformed body. An innocent country boy, he didn't seem to understand what causes what and how long it takes.

But Genya's department could tally the months, even though they knew nothing of what had happened to Genya, who never made a secret of anything, and who was much loved and trusted by her colleagues. Toward the end, one of her colleagues, Artem Mikhailovich, Genya's devoted admirer, took Dima aside and informed him that soon he was going to become a father. A child was going to have a child. Dima beamed his usual smile. For the last time Genya passed through the cafeteria like a yacht, white with blue shadows under her eyes, but Dima still noticed nothing. All May he was gone, studying for the final exams at his extension school. He came back for a month and then disappeared again, to stand his university entrance exams.

In the middle of August he appeared again. Artem stopped him in the corridor and informed Dima he was a father to a son. Here's the address.

Three of Genya's colleagues went to the hospital to greet her at the gate, in accordance with tradition. The department's head, Svetlana, carried flowers, vodka, and cake for the nurses. Artem carried a passel of baby clothes. Dasha carried Genya's personal items. All three were pleased: their mom was no worse than others. They gave everything to the attending nurse and sat down on the porch beside a small crowd of someone's country relatives. Among grandmas in kerchiefs and uncles in cloth caps they spotted the shining Dima with a bouquet of gladioli—it was his family, it turned out. Finally Genya herself appeared with a nurse.

Dima received the baby from the nurse's arms and presented it to his family. Grandmas took a long look and proclaimed, "Dima's!" The uncle produced a bottle and plastic cups from his sack, and everyone drank to the baby's health. Then Genya took the child, waved everyone good-bye, and departed in a cab with a girlfriend. Genya's colleagues and Dima's confused relatives began to walk to the subway.

Dima was beaming; he told Svetlana his college exams had gone well.

A year passed. Genya returned to work. Times were hard. The nanny consumed Genya's entire salary, while Genya subsisted on bread and potatoes and dressed in hand-me-downs. Like many impoverished women she gained a lot of weight. At work she no longer smiled and always tried to leave early. Dima, skinny as a stick, was still on the floor below, working full-time and studying at night. Despite being overworked, he visited little Egor every Saturday, sitting by his crib and watching over him. He slept in the kitchen. His family was dirt-poor, it turned out, and both brother and uncle drank heavily. The uncle soon died. Before Dima finished his six-year college marathon, his brother died, too, also from moonshine poisoning. Only a single aunt was left, and Dima stayed with her in her two-room apartment in Moscow. He was a full editor now, with a college degree. Genya, who had long given up the unaffordable nanny, sent the boy to a boarding preschool, where he stayed Monday through Friday. Every Friday night Dima picked him up and brought him home to Genya. He stayed with them on weekends. On Mondays he took the boy back to his school.

Little Egor called Dima *Papa*. He had both papa and mama, like other children. When the boy was to go to first grade, Dima moved his family to the apartment bequeathed to him by his aunt, whose crutches were still standing in a corner. In spite of the smell of frugal poverty, the apartment was clean, with freshly washed floors, homespun runners, and a white cloth on the kitchen table. Little Egor fell in love with his new home, where he had his own little room and a real desk, which papa had found and fixed for him. Genya quit her old job and began selling potted plants at an outdoor market. Dima was admitted to graduate school and picked up some teaching there; in addition, he tutored high school students. They had a small house in the country, Dima's old family nest, where they spent summer weekends and where Genya grew her plants. She rented out her studio apartment.

They never fought. Occasionally Dima drank himself unconscious—the legacy of generations of alcoholics—but Genya knew how to end his binges. In a brilliant move she saved some money and bought him a secondhand car. Dima spent all his free time under that car, fixing and tuning. Now they could travel to the country in comfort, in their own vehicle, instead of a packed commuter train with a sweaty crowd and their luggage.

Is that it? Not quite. First: Genya never married Dima. Second: Although life had hardened Dima and Genya to the strength of steel, little Egor grew into a softhearted boy without will or ambition. One could see in him the ghosts of Dima's male ancestors—useless, sweet-natured drunks—while on his mother's side the story of his conception foretold frivolity and random liaisons.

Sobered and grim, mother and father looked back on their few minutes of half-naked passion on the cramped kitchen sofa, that sinful, impure moment when their child was conceived. What will become of him? the poor parents asked themselves as they disciplined little Egor, who always smiled and gave away his possessions and longed for friendship and kisses and hugs. After punishments he often cried in his little room and then threw himself on the necks of his only family, his only loved ones, his two grave deities—Papa and Mama. He'd weep and forgive, while they froze in a grim foreboding.

Father and Mother

Where do you live, light-footed Tanya? In what little apartment with white curtains have you built a nest for yourself and your little ones? Quick and resourceful, you find time for everything, and fear of tomorrow never disturbs your sleep.

In what pits of misery this miracle of efficiency grew, this oldest girl in a family of many daughters and a single boy, whom Tanya's mother carried at her breast to the final days of her marriage when she would run after her husband almost every morning to prevent him from escaping to his so-called job? Tanya's mother was filled with despair; again he was escaping her clutches. She gathered her last reserves of strength and chased him with the baby in her arms just to knock the cap off his head with her free hand—all this in view of the neighbors, other military families, who had witnessed dozens of such scenes.

The mother was sick with hatred for her husband, for that scoundrel who betrayed the family daily. Every night he returned home to rock the youngest child, but even this innocent gesture she interpreted as an admission of guilt, a sham confirmation of his fatherhood to which, she felt, he had no right. They almost tore the baby in half. The children seemed little more than material evidence of her suffering and inhuman labor, which her husband daily trampled into dirt. During her ravings he shook with fear that the neighbors would hear, but the neighbors in that small military town had long been aware. She had told them everything, and how the wives pitied her, called her intimately Petrovna and advised her to go to his Party supervisor since things were so bad.

Still the father stayed, came home every night with peaceful intentions and a blithe expression on his face, always at eleven sharp, never earlier; he had never in his life come home earlier—it was his iron-clad rule. And every night he found the same tableau: none of the children was asleep; his tearful wife was sitting up in bed, the youngest at her breast. If the father attempted to put the kids to bed in his gentle way, Tanya's mother pulled them away, screaming that no one was going to sleep, since that was what he wanted. Let everyone admire their so-called father—fresh from somebody's bed where he was kissing God knows what with his filthy mouth, and now he wanted to kiss his innocent daughters and jump into their beds, and so on.

The squalor of that household was beyond description, because the mother did her housework sloppily, saving her energy for the high point of her day: for eleven at night, which bled into midnight and later, so the children got no sleep and couldn't get up in the morning for school. The mother went further in her sacred rage, appearing at the officers' mess with the little one and kicking her husband as he walked out the door, as if to disprove the conventional wisdom that such methods never brought anyone's husband back (quite the opposite). Leaving behind her children unfed, she'd chase her husband through town, screaming the most horrible things—that, say, she had found bloody rags tucked in a hole in the wall and that Tanya had had a miscarriage by her father.

No one understood what Tanya's mother was

hoping to achieve with these displays; possibly all she really wanted was to shatter the illusion her husband had been trying to create for the children's sake, with his nonchalance and conciliatory manner. Of course the mother knew that people had sympathy for her husband and wanted to protect him from her. Once, someone warned him that she was on her way to the store, where she knew he would be buying small presents for her and the girls (it was Women's Day, when even little girls expected at least a flower from their fathers), and he managed to escape through the back door.

Despite all this ugliness, a baby was born almost every year, and the last one, the only boy, was born just six months before the father finally left. What inspired their conjugal embraces, how and when father and mother became one, was a mystery to everyone—even to the smartest in the family, Tanya, who watched her parents closely.

The mother wouldn't give up her attempts to humiliate her husband, and she sank deeper and deeper into shame while he maintained some semblance of family cohesion at all costs and refused to be kicked out on her terms. Eventually the least determined combatant stopped caring about the outcome of this endless rout and walked away, exhausted. Tanya's father was transferred to another garrison, with damage, it was whispered, to his career. So he had every reason not to show his face to his long-suffering family. He settled in a new place with some woman who was said to be much more common than Petrovna.

Tanya stayed at home one more year, until she turned seventeen. Then she was noticed by Victor, an electrician in town on a temporary contract, who saw right away what treasure had fallen into his hands. The first night, on the way back from the dance hall, she agreed to move away with him, and the following morning they left, even though the mother had told her she couldn't cope without Tanya and that the children would suffer. "Enough," Tanya (reportedly) said. "I've had enough." And she set off with her older (twenty-four-year-old) electrician and never once looked back.

Everything that happened to her afterward—homelessness, then a landlady who drank nothing but kefir and tried to hang herself every March but was rescued by her son—all this adversity she considered happiness, and not a shadow of doubt or despair ever touched her.

The Impulse

What terrible fits she threw, this proud fighter
for love! It's incredible what she went through. Take,
for example, her departing husband's good-bye punch
that knocked one of her front teeth inward (they
managed to pull it back out). Take her children: the
daughter would hang up after ten seconds of Dasha's
sobbing; the son, well, he had to stay with her, with
his mother—there was nowhere to go. They survived
in her moldy shack outside the city, the mother and
her young son. The boy went to the village school;
they bought their groceries at the understocked local
store: potato chips, ice cream, and frozen pizza, on

occasion bread and butter—there was nothing more on offer. That's where she and her son stayed year-round except for the time she chased her lover, the light of her life, who happened to be a most ordinary man—stingy and not particularly young. She shaved her head from all the stress, but everything looked becoming on her: her permanent fatigue and near emaciation, her cracked lips, shaved head, dilated eyes.

Until recently Alyosha's life had been well and good. He had a wife, who was a foreign national, a son in college, a pleasant apartment in a comfortable European country, a summerhouse in Lithuania, and, in addition to all that, any number of quick liaisons during business trips. (His fling with Dasha began with a quick roll on a hotel bed during one such trip.) Then, the following summer, his company sent him to Moscow on a long assignment and rented him an apartment. That was where Dasha visited him, leaving her young son alone in the shack. During Dasha's absences the boy subsisted on ice cream and frozen pizza, which he and his village friends would try to heat up on his father's old grill. Dasha didn't mind; on the contrary, she was proud of her son's resourcefulness. (Here are some potatoes for you, Son; try to cook them as well!) On each of her passionate visits, however, Dasha had to roll out of bed in time to catch the last train back to the shack. How the two lovers howled and wept at those partings!

Suddenly the skies brightened. Dasha managed to find a spot in a summer camp for her son. As soon as the boy left, she dashed to the city to announce to her "husband" that for the next twenty-four days they belonged to only each other. (She did this in person because he wouldn't answer his phone.) She was planning to surprise her beloved in their love nest with a romantic dinner. But upon reaching the front door, she discovered that the key to his apartment was missing from her key ring.

Dasha stared wildly at Alyosha's windows. His balcony was directly above the first-floor balcony, which was protected by iron bars. She and Alyosha used to wonder why anyone would want to live imprisoned behind those ugly bars. They had decided that potential burglars could climb up them to get to *their* balcony, which meant they, too, should install bars, and so should the people above them, and so forth. That's how they would joke, these carefree owners of nothing, who had no property in the city or anywhere near it except for Dasha's crumbling country shack. The shack, it was true, was in an upscale area. Here we must point out that this Dasha wasn't exactly broke; we are not talking about a penniless divorcée with a child—not at all. Dasha was making more money in her job than her cuckolded husband or even this Alyosha, her most recent passion. She only appeared to be a charity case; in fact, ground had been broken on the site of her new mansion.

But now this successful Dasha felt she must enter her lover's house. Who knew when he'd be back? She couldn't just sit and wait, this impulsive nymph, could she? She scrambled up the bars of the first-floor balcony and hopped up to the second. Alyosha's balcony door was unlocked.

Dasha stepped into the hall with delicious anticipation. She was going to get a drink of water from the kitchen when something caught her eye: a semi-unpacked suitcase in the bedroom, a purse by the bed, and the bed itself, which looked like the site of a recent sexual conquest—Dasha noticed fresh milky spots on a rumpled towel.

So, Alyosha had just slept with another woman. From the kitchen came sounds of cooking—the slut was obviously making use of Dasha's new porcelain chopping board—and also of an intimate conversation between the slut and Alyosha. The slut was making herself at home here—and not for the first time, that was clear.

Dasha was hysterical. She stumbled into the

kitchen, choking on her snot and tears, appealing to her "husband" for reassurance, the very husband who had just screwed another woman. She screamed at the terrified hag, who held a chopping knife in midair. Looking through her tears, Dasha stretched out her arms toward the blurry figure, the pale, frightened Alyosha, who could be heard muttering something.

Her performance that day was the cry of a betrayed, rebellious soul. Never again did she produce a monologue of such force. She gave one final moan, spun around, and flew out of the apartment. Once outside, she ran blindly through the traffic to the highway, and there she halted to flag down a car with a shaking hand. This was where her impulse let go of her, finally, and she was overtaken by Alyosha, who got into the car with her and rode out to her shack— for good.

It was his wife, he told her. She had arrived without warning.

So the wife had arrived, the phone had been disconnected, and the door to the apartment had been locked with a special safety button to trap burglars inside—only Dasha and Alyosha knew about it. On her way out, Dasha had unlocked this clever button without thinking. The wife, however, couldn't have known about it; it must have been Alyosha who locked it against Dasha's arrival. Also, what could have happened to her key? How could it have disappeared from the ring?

In all their life together she didn't ask her husband these questions, not once.

Hallelujah, Family!

This, in short, is what happened.

1. A young girl worked as a secretary during the day and took classes at night. She came from a respectable family, although her mother had a certain history:

2. She was the illegitimate child of two mothers and one father. You see,

3. there were two sisters: one was married, the other was just fifteen, and she got pregnant by her brother-in-law, who hanged himself while she gave birth to a daughter she hated.

4. That daughter grew up, got married, and had a baby, a daughter.

5. That daughter was our little secretary/student, Alla. Our Alla began to go out with men as soon as she turned fifteen. Her mother cried and scolded her, but nothing helped, and the mother began to lose her mind. In addition to which she was diagnosed with an illness

6. that promised immobility. She and Alla got along horribly, because

7. Alla was raised by her grandmother (3), who hated her daughter, Alla's mother, and who at thirty-five took her little granddaughter to live with her in a provincial town where she shared a house with her uncle, a much older man.

8. Who knew what lay behind the cohabitation of a fifty-year-old uncle and his niece, who were the only ones left from a large family after all the wars, arrests, divorces, forced and unforced deaths?

9. Then they were joined by little Alla. The girl lived in fear that her mother, Elena, would eventually take her back, and once had a nightmare in which her mother was an evil witch.

10. But nothing could be done: her mother and father missed her, and soon after this nightmare the girl went back to Moscow, where she entered

first grade. Poor Elena: the middle link in this chain, hated on both sides—by her child and by her mother.

11. Then Alla, unmarried, gave birth. Her mother, stooped over, shuffled around, washing diapers, cooking, cleaning. All this she did grudgingly, as there was no money in the house. Elena lived on her invalid's pension; her husband had died, and Alla wasn't working, having just given birth to a daughter, Nadya. Elena's memory of her terrible past—of her illegitimate father's death in the noose, of her quiet teenage mother— weighed Elena down, and she nagged and nagged poor Alla, who'd huddle by the baby's crib and try not to cry.

12. Little Nadya had a father, but he lived with Alla only sporadically, considering her used-up material. He had made her pregnant twice, and when it happened the third time, Victor—who saw himself not as a future father but simply as a facilitator of another abortion—put Alla in a cab and directed the driver to the same hospital. He told the driver to wait, walked Alla to the ward, and pecked her on the cheek. This time, though, he left before she changed into the sterile hospital robe, so he didn't take her street clothes from her.

13. Alla spent the night in the ward, thinking—that

she was twenty-five, that Victor had left her, that all her future held were random liaisons with married men. As morning approached, Alla hugged her belly and felt she had a family, that she was no longer alone.

14. She put on her street clothes and left the hospital.

15. Victor never called. Alla was taking her exams; she was a good worker, and her boss had agreed to promote her to engineer before she got her diploma. As for her belly, nobody noticed anything; her colleagues decided that skinny girl had finally blossomed. At the same time, an attractive intern started at the office and assumed Alla's old secretarial position.

16. Alla did mention to her boss, at a good moment, that she and her mother were in bad shape; that they needed extra money for the mother's medications.

17. But she never revealed her pregnancy, neither to him nor to Victor, whom she ran into during finals. The rogue took one look at Alla's swollen breasts and invited her to his place after the exam.

18. Alla politely greeted Victor's mother, Nina Petrovna, whom she'd always liked. (It's not uncommon for estranged daughters to look for mother figures in older women.) Nina, too, was

well disposed to Alla: she was the only girl Victor brought to the apartment openly.

19. In his tiny shoebox of a room, Victor entered Alla like she was his old home. Everything was familiar—the smell, the skin; only the body itself was different, and Victor couldn't get enough of it. You just don't age, he kept telling her in the dark. Finally they went out into the living room. Victor made some tea, and that's when Alla announced

20. that things had changed. Victor was sure Alla's transformation was attributable to a new affair, and he chewed his cookie regretfully.

21. That's right, Alla said. I've met someone, and I love him as much as I love you.

22. Ah, well, Victor sighed, and kept on chewing.

23. We are going to have a baby.

24. What? Another baby? Victor felt sleepy and confused. He just wanted to be left alone.

25. Then it occurred to him that perhaps Alla knew how to determine pregnancy right after the act—girls these days knew all kinds of things. When did you get knocked up? he croaked.

26. In September!

27. In September? I see. . . .

28. She explained what had happened at the hospital, but he refused to believe her. Two weeks

later he proposed to the daughter of a nice family that lived in a house with clean floors and polished furniture. The girl resembled Marguerite from *Faust*: blond hair, blue eyes, endless braid.

29. However, some friends informed Nina Petrovna that Alla was pregnant by her son, and so she boycotted the wedding, which was held a month later.

30. Victor must have sensed some danger from the beautiful Alla, from her full breasts, her moist mouth, silky hair—he must have sensed that this gorgeous body was meant to seduce him, as Alla's fifteen-year-old grandmother, consciously or unconsciously, had seduced her brother-in-law, who thereby became the husband of two sisters and so quickly dispatched himself.

31. Victor wanted to find refuge in his ideal Marguerite, but Alla's belly grew remorselessly, and on his birthday Alla presented it to him, like a gift.

32. To cheat fate, Victor signed a three-year contract at a big industrial site two thousand miles away. He reckoned that in three years they'd all forget about him, including Alla, who'd find herself a husband. It was like a temporary suicide, he thought, a thing that everyone desires at some

point—to step out for a while, then come back to see what happened.

33. Victor partied all night before his departure, and Alla was there, too, at his mother's invitation, ballooned like a drowned corpse, with cracked black lips. By the morning he had second thoughts about his impending three-year death and lost some of his nerve—but what could he do? Life in his hometown with swollen Alla appeared no less terrible, for only teenagers are drawn to everything that reminds them of their earliest days. Besides, Victor was in love again, with a superbly skinny and lithe contortionist named Zhanna, whose amateur act he'd caught in a nearby town where he'd gone to escape his amiable but unyielding mother. After the performance Victor slipped out and waited for Zhanna by the back entrance. He walked her to the bus, took down her address, and the next day met her in Moscow at her dorm. They took a walk through a park where trees were beginning to turn, and Victor's only reward was a kiss on her bony little hand.

34. With Zhanna's address in his wallet, and shedding bitter tears, Victor was dragged by one of his buddies to the train station.

35. At the industrial site, Victor shared a single room

with a young married couple. They arrived a day
after he did and were embarrassed to find him lying on a bed in their assigned room. But it wasn't
a mistake: housing was tight, and with this couple Victor witnessed the entire cycle of child-
making, up to the day the young mother returned
from the hospital with her baby. The baby was
covered with a septic rash—his whole little head
felt like a cactus due to the tiny bumps. His
parents bowed before this new catastrophe and
tended to him day and night until he got better.
Victor did what he could, didn't sleep either,
and ran around to various offices trying to get
them alternate accommodations. Then one day
he stopped by their place to pick up the couple's
paperwork, and the young mother, who was trying to nurse, looked at him with such intense
hatred that he thought, What am I doing? If this
is death, there is no room for me here.

36. He'd accumulated several notes from Zhanna as
well as a number of letters from Alla with pictures of little Nadya, who was a replica of Victor
plus dimples and curls. His mother also wrote—
that Alla's life with her mentally ill mother (2–5)
was becoming unbearable, that the crazy woman
had put washing detergent in Nadya's cereal and

wouldn't let Nina Petrovna see her own grand-daughter.

37. On receiving this news Victor felt uneasy, almost scared, for until now the fact that he could return home anytime made his life at the industrial site a little more bearable. Now, he realized his mother would probably move little Nadya to their apartment, and also Alla, so there wouldn't be anywhere for him to go.

38. Then he caught his wretched roommate looking at him as though she wished him dead, and suddenly he understood why these wretched people were so indifferent to his attempts to find them a separate room: all they wanted was for him to disappear, to let them be; a separate room he needed really for himself, so he could bring there Tanya, Galya, and Liuba.

39. Zhanna had stopped writing and wouldn't answer his calls. Victor spent half the night at the post office in the nearest town trying to reach her, and in the end fell asleep on a chair inside the phone booth. The first bus back to the industiral site was at four in the morning. On his way through the dark he upset a basin full of water for the child who woke with a wail; his parents crawled out of bed, blind with exhaus-

tion; Victor tried to collect the water; the baby kept wailing. . . .

40. In the morning Victor went to the personnel office and handed in his resignation on the grounds that in eleven months he hadn't received housing. Zhanna was seducing him with her silence.

41. I guess I'll marry her, he decided with tears in his eyes. Nina Petrovna had sent him a telegram that romantic Marguerite had divorced him in absentia.

42. Free at last! he thought happily, and pictured Zhanna's face.

43. Although it was a bit strange, he considered, that Nina Petrovna had reported the news so openly in a telegram.

44. Two weeks later Zhanna was scheduled to meet him at the station. In fact, the whole gang was there.

45. It was August, and the small train platforms outside Moscow were filled with brightly dressed vacationers. Victor was peering through a dusty coach window, trying to make out Zhanna's silhouette, but instead he saw two women and a stroller with a rather big baby, and one of the women was crying, covering her face. Nina Petrovna wasn't crying—she lifted the baby and held it in front of her like a shield.

My Little One

———

Give Her to Me

This Christmas story has a sad beginning and a happy ending. It begins in March with a certain Misha, a struggling composer from the provinces. He'd written a dozen children's songs and two symphonies, Fifth and Tenth, so named as a joke. Misha survived by moonlighting at clubs with various bands. Onstage he wore a lace blouse and a fake bust, like Jack Lemmon in *Some Like It Hot*. That spring he was hired to write a score for a senior show at a drama school, an assigment for which he got paid by the hour, next to nothing. He wrote in his kitchen, at night, while his wife's family, who unanimously despised Misha, slept nearby.

Now enters our second character, an extremely thin and unattractive senior at the drama school. Karpenko (her last name) was one of those unfortunate creatures forced to compensate for their appearance with a pleasant disposition and a carefree attitude. She was accepted to the school for her undeniable talent, but a successful actress needs other qualities—no one quite knows exactly what: feminine charm, perhaps, or steely ambition. Karpenko was as humble as a beggar. While her classmates rode off with their admirers in expensive cars, she inspired interest solely from her graying professors of voice and dance. Although she practiced at the barre every day, her froglike appearance condemned her to roles of servants and old ladies who neither sing nor dance.

Luckily Karpenko was assigned the part of a horse, with a little dancing, in the senior show *Getting Matches*, which was based on a Finnish novel. Her voice professor insisted that Karpenko perform one short song. As there were no songs in the play, Karpenko and Misha met in an empty auditorium to write one. Misha composed a catchy tune, and Karpenko assembled some lyrics. Misha, impressed, batted his eyes and shook his head in disbelief.

Karpenko, blind with happiness, flew to her dorm. No one had ever looked at her with such admiration. She'd grown up in the Far North, in a family of political exiles. Her ancestors owned country estates and danced in their own ballrooms, but now the family counted as many as four children, the mother worked as a nurse, and they all lived off their vegetable patch. The Karpenko women were known for their reticence and regal beauty, but the little froggy took after her father, a bush pilot who left his family when he retired. A little later Karpenko departed for the capital to become an actress, and her mother seemed to forget her. They didn't meet for five years. To get from the capital to her village, one had to ride the train for seven days, then a bus for thirty-six hours, then another bus, which sometimes didn't run, for seven more. Froggy's letters went unanswered for three, four months.

Misha and Karpenko had a fruitful collaboration, and at the end of March the play was performed before the faculty and students. The maestro praised the part of the horse, especially her tap dance, and the voice professor bored everyone with a lecture on how to teach singing to students with insufficient talent. The audience loved the horse and yelled "Bravo!" Misha and Karpenko, both exhausted, took a long time packing their music and texts. By the time they finished, the subway was no longer running. They climbed up to the attic, and there, on an old mattress, Misha betrayed his wife for the first time, and Karpenko became a woman. That summer their play was performed at a student festival in Finland, where Karpenko was named the best supporting actress. Her certificate, written in Finnish, was displayed in the department.

The maestro selected a new professional company. Municipal authorities allowed them to use a warehouse on the city outskirts. The maestro's old friend Mr. Osip Tartiuk became the company's general manager. He proceeded to cast about for a new play, as Finnish-singing horses couldn't be expected to attract much interest in that blue-collar neighborhood or among the theater's municipal benefactors. Karpenko didn't win the job. Tartiuk liked his women fat; on every heavy derriere he commented, "What a centaur!" At the banquets, after the third glass, he liked to confess he was interested in only a large butt.

The unemployed Karpenko tried this and that, and finally got hired to sell vegetables two days a week at a big outdoor food market. Her situation was dire—she was four months pregnant.

She rented a cot in the kitchen of an alcoholic couple who were themselves children and grandchildren of alcoholics. Pasha was the husband's name. His enormous wife was called Elephant. Their two sons were in jail. In the summer the couple paraded in shorts and lavender panamas donated by some international aid organization, and hunted promising spots for cans and bottles like experienced mushroom pickers. In the winter Pasha and Elephant impersonated blind beggars. They stashed their equipment—dark glasses, two canes, and for some reason a dog's leash—under Karpenko's cot, behind her suitcase.

Luckily Elephant never cooked; she visited the kitchen where Karpenko lived only by mistake, when she wandered the apartment on the verge of delirium tremens. At night the couple relaxed in the company of select neighbors. Their room filled up with the local elite—prominent alcoholics and their girlfriends in various stages of decline. The excluded spent the night banging on their broken-down door. These soirees invariably ended in fights that were occasionally interrupted by sleepy patrolmen.

Every day, Karpenko scrubbed the toilet and the tub; she replaced the broken glass in the kitchen door with thick plywood. At night she stuffed her ears with soft wax, like Odysseus on his ship when he sailed past the sirens.

Once, she dropped by the new theater dorms

and left some fruit for the girls. Just in case, she also left her new address. Misha soon came to see her. She had nothing for him to eat beyond some potatoes and carrots, which she was allowed to bring home from the market where she worked. Misha stayed the night, but he couldn't sleep because of the drunken screaming and banging; in the morning he scrambled away as soon as the subway started up. Karpenko, who hadn't mentioned her pregnancy, didn't expect him back.

Three days later Misha reappeared with a keyboard: he had written a score to a musical. While he performed his score for Karpenko, the landlords and their visitors gathered outside the kitchen door and treated themselves to an impromptu dance party, obviously approving of Misha's music. Karpenko, inspired, pulled out her most precious possession, an old typewriter, and wrote a play.

At that time theaters were interested only in plays translated from Italian. Misha and Karpenko invented an author, "Alidada Nektolai, as translated from the Italian by U. Karpui." Their cast included a philandering lawyer and his skinny wife; the wife's girlfriend, who slept with the lawyer and was married to the mayor; the mayor and his mafia friends, named Kafka, Lorca, and Petrarch; and so on. The heroine was a beautiful aspiring singer named Gallina Bianca. Misha observed that Karpenko would never get the lead, and so they created a character for her, a television executive named Julietta Mamasina who spoke entirely in Elephant's morning monologues.

One day Elephant returned home covered in bruises and carrying a box of powdered milk that she'd discovered in an expensive supermarket's Dumpster—the scene of many a fight over discarded goods. Pasha and Elephant sent a few packages to the market with Karpenko, but it seemed no one wanted to buy expired milk, and Elephant lost interest in the box. (Her guests did try to mix the powder with vodka, but the combination made them itchy.) The milk was left for the undernourished Karpenko, who added to her diet of raw carrots and beets, cottage cheese, and one boiled egg a serving of oatmeal cooked with milk.

The play was retyped, the songs recorded, and the arrangement copyrighted. Misha went to see the theater's general manager, Mr. Osip Tartiuk, who received the play with indifference. Three days later, however, Tartiuk invited Misha to a staff meeting, where he sang and played his heart out. The play was accepted on the spot. Everyone was excited, until Misha announced that Alidada Nektolai demanded four thousand dollars for his play. Osip nearly lost his voice.

"We are young! We are poor!" he squeaked.

"Nektolai says that every company tells him they are young and poor. You want the play, pay up. Otherwise, there's a long line."

Osip cautiously inquired if there were other options.

"Another option would be to pay the translator directly, half that amount."

"But I know her! She's a regular centaur!" Here Osip gestured with his hands. "An ass like hers . . . she'll give us a discount!"

"I seriously doubt it. Theaters like yours are a dime a dozen, and they all want her."

"We'll offer her a thousand dollars! A whole thousand!"

"If she gets a thousand, then so do I, as the author of the score."

"Who needs your score? We'll put some sound-track together!" Osip glared at Misha's poor little keyboard.

"Translator Karpui insists her lyrics and my music stay together," Misha piped up nervously. "It's a musical—don't you get it? Every theater in Moscow makes money on musicals except you in your dump!"

Osip looked deflated. He promised Misha an appropriate solution and pulled him into his office.

After a lengthy discussion Misha was promised $1,500 and, for Karpenko, a room in the theater dorm, a part in the play, and a permanent position with the company.

"What's going on between you and this Karpenko, young man? Has your wife been informed?" Osip asked suspiciously.

"We are getting a divorce," Misha blurted out, surprising himself.

"And do you actually know this Karpui?"

"Karpui is Karpenko—she wrote the play herself. We hold copyright to both the play and the music."

"You can shut up now! This Karpenko and her play are worth maybe a hundred dollars on a good day. If you want, I'll make her a janitor; we need one in the theater."

"Great! We'll sell the play to the best theater in Moscow for my price!"

"Two hundred?"

At this moment the maestro walked in, beaming, and announced he'd never seen such enthusiasm among the actors about a new play. "I can see it onstage! And you"—here the maestro called Misha several names—"are in my way with your music!"

Enraged, normally meek Misha lost his compo-sure and demanded a thousand each—immediately and in dollars, not rubles.

"Immediately? I can't," Osip replied peevishly.

"The translator and I will come in on Monday."

"On Monday I can't, either. Mmm . . . make it Wednesday."

"So on Wednesday you'll meet my conditions, right?"

"Look, Misha!" Osip started yelling again. "I need a janitor! Renovations are almost over; who's going to clean up this mess?"

A pause.

"By the way," Osip announced to the confused maestro, "your former student Karpenko has just returned from Finland, where she's been working in television."

"From Finland? That's where she was! Suddenly my student disappears. . . . So she'll play Gallina Bianca; she'll be perfect! In the first act she's a skinny little thing; in the second she'll have big boobs and high heels—"

"Actually, she wanted to play Julietta Mama-sina," interrupted Misha.

"Who cares what she wants!" screamed Osip. "Fine, let her play already," he finished quietly.

At the dorm, Karpenko moved into a room belonging to two girls who had been forced to move into a double, which now became a triple. The aggravation intensified as new parts were assigned. Oh theater, the snake pit of snake pits! The question suddenly arose as to why Misha was living in the dorm without any registration, while the rest of them had to pay extra for gas and electricity. Also, did Misha's wife know what was happening? Somebody should inform her. The wife and their ten-year-old son once came to see Misha, waiting for him until the last train. God knows how Osip found out, but he warned Misha, and he and Karpenko hid at the Domodedovo airport.

The new season opened with previews. Karpenko made sure her costume provided room for her growing belly. Fake bust, miniskirt, red wig, high boots on flat soles—comic in the extreme. The premiere was a great success. Julietta sang off-key and danced like an elephant, a model for future starlets. In the dorm everyone knew about Karpenko's pregnancy and positioned themselves to take over her part.

A few weeks later Osip Tartiuk stopped by Karpenko's room. Karpenko was lying on the bed. Misha, wearing headphones, was bent over his keyboard.

"So what are we going to do?" Osip inquired. "When are you due? We need time to replace you!"

"December 31."

"So what do we do? We have two weeks left."

"Let Misha do it. He knows the part. You don't have any actresses who can play it."

Tartiuk looked stunned.

"Misha!" Karpenko shook him by the shoulder. Misha took off his headphones. Karpenko ordered him to change into Julietta's costume. Twisting his arms like a flamenco dancer, Misha squeezed into it. He looked beyond funny: a miniskirt, enormous breasts, a butt like two watermelons, and, under red curls, an unshaved sallow mug with a huge *schnobel*.

"A regular centaur.... Well, well. Have a safe delivery. Ciao!" Osip left. Karpenko lay in bed, swallowed by her belly. Misha saw nothing notable in her swollen body. He was used to large women—his previous wife was the biggest centaur in the pack. A week later he took over Karpenko's role.

On December 31 the show ended at nine thirty. Misha called Karpenko's phone, but no one answered. He tried the dorm; the line was hopelessly busy. He changed, threw flowers into a cab, and arrived at the dorm ahead of everyone else. The phone's receiver was lying on the floor. Their door was open. The floor was wet. Everything in the room was turned upside down. What had happened here? Where could she have gone in such a condition? She had talked about doing some tests . . . He checked under the bed. There, by the wall, he found her purse. A passport, mobile phone, her medical history . . . Okay, let's see: Nadezhda A. Karpenko, pregnant, due December 31. Pregnant? He dialed the medical emergency number. An hour later he found out that Nadezhda Karpenko hadn't been admitted to any hospital, including any maternity wards. Misha collapsed on the floor. Suddenly he heard explosions in the street. New Year's fireworks.

Karpenko had dragged herself to a nearby maternity ward. She knocked for a long time. Finally a tipsy nurse admitted her. "I'm not feeling well," Karpenko whispered. The nurse, who didn't look too good either, announced, "Lissssssssten . . . ," sounding exactly like Elephant, but she couldn't finish the sentence and stumbled off. Karpenko lay down on the bench and closed her eyes. A fiery canon ball was rolling in her belly, trying to make more room. A young woman in white loomed over her. Karpenko managed to recite her lines: "Couldn't find my papers, somebody took my purse, everything was there—my phone, my passport, my medical history. . . . Had some cash in my coat but couldn't get a cab. . . . My father flew away. . . . No one wants us, no one. . . ." Someone kept asking her name and date of birth. "I'm an actress," was all she could manage before passing out.

She awoke in a large room with tiled walls that looked like a swimming pool. People in white masks stood over her.

"Hey, you! Open your eyes," she heard. "There you go. Are you planning to push or what? What's your name?"

"Karp . . ."

"Lovely name. Hey, don't you die on us—don't ruin our New Year!"

The pain came. Her body was turning inside out. Inhuman torture began.

"Push, push! Okay, stop for now!"

She felt them stab her with a knife and then twist it. They'll cut the baby!

"Don't, don't stab me!" she screamed in her stage voice.

"Calm down. It's the baby, not us. The baby's pulling you apart. There, I can see the crown!"

Suddenly she heard a low sound like a train whistle.

"Mom, look up! It's a girl! A real beauty! Somebody, give her salts. What's your last name?"

"Karpenko. Nadezhda Alexandrovna Karpenko."

"Finally! Now take a good look: it's a girl—see for yourself; we don't want any complaints afterward!"

Eyes over white gauze masks. Laughing. One of them was holding a little baby doll, tiny, unwashed. All crinkled up, crying. She's cold! Never before had Karpenko felt such heart-wrenching pity.

"Rejoice, Mom! Such a big, beautiful gal! A happy New Year!"

"Just give her to me. . . . Give her to me, please. . . . Just give her to me. . . ."

Milgrom

A girl is sewing herself a dress for the first time. She has bought three yards of cheap gingham (barely more than a ruble per yard), but it's surprisingly pretty, black with bright circles, like a nighttime carnival.

This girl is a penniless college student. She has broken out of her schoolgirl shell, literally so— she managed to make a new skirt out of her old school uniform. The skirt came out messy, crooked, and off-center, but that's the end of the uniform, anyway.

Nor did the skirt turn out to be fit for spring. It's

May, the hottest spring in memory, and still there's nothing to wear.

So the girl, following the "Sewing Ourselves" page from a women's magazine spread out before her (chest measurements, front panels), tries to make the dress herself and fails utterly.

The dress is lost, as are three rubles' worth of fabric. Her monthly stipend at the college is only twenty-three rubles.

Here the mom intervenes. Her whole life, Mom relied on a seamstress, but then difficult times befell her; her girl turned eighteen, and she stopped receiving child support.

The seamstress is out, and Mom considers what to do, except here's the problem: there's no money.

There's no money, the girl is eighteen, it's a hot May (the kind you feel maybe once every hundred years), and there are exams to take. But her daughter can't go outside. She's lying behind the wardrobe—that's where her cot is—weeping and moaning like a puppy.

So Mom calls her wise older friend, Regina, a Polish Jewess from the clan of the Moscow wives (that is to say, the new wives) of the Third International. In the thirties this whole communist contingent left the countries where it lived underground, came to the USSR via mountains and seas, remarried in Moscow, and then went up to heaven from their labor camps. Regina had served her time in Karaganda, was rehabilitated after the war, got back her old apartment on Gorky Street. The girl's mother, who'd also seen some things in her time, latched onto her to learn about life. Regina was a good friend of the girl's mother's mother, who has also been serving her time and is expected to return this spring.

Regina always dresses with Warsaw chic. She's sixty now and still has suitors, and she listens with sympathy to the confused mother of the girl.

Regina has a houseworker named Riva Milgrom. Regina is a European lady; she has soft white hands like an empress, and her house is always in order, as Milgrom makes sure.

That's what she's called: Milgrom—her last name, according to the old Party habit. Milgrom has a Singer sewing machine. The girl walks with the bundle of material through the May heat in her brown wool skirt. We know where the skirt came from—the mother had a dress she wore down until the underarms had sweat stains in the form of half-moons, at which point the dress was bequeathed to the girl, who wore it to school but could never raise her hand in class, her elbows clinging to her sides like a soldier's; it was hell. Finally the top with the sweat stains was cut off, and though the mother protested that it could still become a nice vest, the girl ran out of the apartment and threw it down the trash chute. Still the crooked skirt remained, and that's the skirt she's wearing as she walks clumsily through the heat of May.

Over the skirt, to cover the tear, which was hemmed crookedly with the wrong thread—the hands sewing them were the wrong hands—the girl wears her mother's blouse, which also has sweat stains at the pits, so, again, elbows at her sides like a soldier's.

The girl walks like a draftee, head down, watching her green winter shoes with their thick soles, her elbows at her sides. She passes by Patriarch Ponds; there's a gentle May smell in the air; young men are marching by, observing proud young girls in their new summer dresses.

Milgrom meets her little customer in her room, which is high up, right beneath the scorching Moscow sky—it's practically the attic—and here is quiet Milgrom with her big moist eyes, very white skin, and total absence of teeth. Milgrom looks like an old lady—her nose almost touches her sharp chin.

She opens up her sewing machine, produces a tape measure, and as she records the girl's measurements Milgrom launches into a saga about her darling son, the beautiful Sasha.

Sasha was so beautiful, people on the street would stop and stare; once his picture appeared on a box of chocolates.

The girl looks at the photograph on the wall that Milgrom points out to her: nothing special—a little boy in a sailor's outfit, big black eyes, a thin, elegant nose. The upper lip protrudes like a visor over the lower one. A cute kid with curls, but nothing more. The lips are too thin for an angel's—he has the Milgrom mouth.

At this point in her life the girl not only has no thoughts of children herself, but she also doesn't have an admirer even, not a single suitor, despite all her eighteen years.

For her it's all work, exams, library, cafeteria, shapeless green shoes, and a horrible brown dress with her mother's pit stains.

The girl looks indifferently at the wall and notices another portrait, an enlarged passport photo of a scrawny young officer in an enormous military cap.

That's the same Sasha; now he's all grown-up. While they were measuring her waist and noting it all down and ruefully examining the cut-up fabric, Sasha got married and produced a granddaughter, Asya Milgrom.

Old Milgrom pauses to console the girl and tells

her she's not the only one who's clumsy, that she herself couldn't do anything when she was young—boil an egg or hem a diaper—and then she learned. Life taught her.

At some point during the long and bragging tale of Sasha it's time to go, but the dress stays; it will be finished tomorrow.

Three days later the girl—who wouldn't leave the house in her awful outfit, but who doesn't know how to wash, or iron, or sew anything; all she can do is read through tears in her corner behind the wardrobe—finally pulls herself together and says to her mother, "I'm going to Milgrom's."

"That poor thing," her mother says. "What a miserable life she's had. Her husband dumped her, literally kicked her out of the house, and took away her child, a little boy. First he took Milgrom out of her Lithuanian village—she was a rare beauty, sixteen years old, but she didn't speak any Russian, just Yiddish and Polish—and then he divorced her; you could do that then—with total freedom, he went and divorced her. And he brought another woman to live with him, and told Milgrom to leave. So she left. She was eighteen years old. She nearly went crazy; she spent all her days and nights on the street across from her old window so she could see her child.

Regina found her half-dead, lying on the street—Regina being the protector of all the oppressed, of course. She put her in a hospital, and took her in as her maid—Milgrom used to sleep in the hall. When Regina was arrested, Milgrom apprenticed at a garment factory, earning herself a small pension and a room."

The girl listens to this absentmindedly, then goes to Milgrom's without really understanding what she's been told, and she sees the same little room just under the roof, where the smell of old woolen clothing chokes you in the heat.

Everything melts in the light of the setting sun as Milgrom produces some cups and a teakettle from the kitchen. They drink tea with black salted crackers, the luxury of the poor.

Milgrom once again brags about her son, Sasha, her shining face turned to the photographs on the wall, although the girl thinks, if her mother is telling the truth, where did she get those photographs?

Grown-up Sasha looks back from the wall with a cold, closed-off stare, his cap sticking up like a saddle over his big black eyes. Now he really looks like his mother.

With what tears, with what pleas did Milgrom get those photos from him?

Milgrom sighs contentedly underneath her wailing wall and then announces that little Asya has just lost her first tooth. All the things that everyone else has, Milgrom has them, too.

The girl puts on her dress; looks in the mirror; escapes from that sweet-musty smell, out into the street, the sunset; and walks by countless doors and windows, behind each of which, she thinks, live only Milgroms, Milgroms, Milgroms. She walks in her cool new black dress, and she is seized with happiness, filled with joy. It fills Milgrom, too, who is joyful for her Sasha.

The girl is at the very beginning of her journey. She's walking in a new dress, young men are already looking, and so on. In five years a boy will appear at her door with a bunch of roses he pulled out from a rose bush somewhere during the night. Milgrom is obviously at the end of her journey, but there might come a time when the girl will flash by at the end of Little Bronnaya Street, in a whole new form, carrying in her purse the photographs of her grown-up son, and bragging about him while sitting on a bench by the Patriarch Ponds—but she doesn't dare call him an extra time, and as for him, he's too busy to call.

The black dress shimmies down Little Bronnaya, which is wide and still filled with light, underneath the setting sun, and that's it now, the day is burning its last, and Milgrom, eternal Milgrom, sits in her little pensioner's room like a guard at the museum of her own life, where there is nothing at all but a timid love.

The Story of Clarissa

Until Clarissa turned seventeen not a single soul admired or noticed her—in that respect she was not unlike Cinderella or the Ugly Duckling. At an age when most girls are sensitive to beauty and look for it everywhere, Clarissa was a primitive, absentminded creature who stared openmouthed at trivial things, like the teacher wiping off the blackboard, and God knows what thoughts ran through her head. In her last year at school, she was involved in a fight. It was provoked by an insult Clarissa believed had been directed at her. In fact, the word wasn't directed at Clarissa or anyone in particular (very few words had been said about her), but instead of explaining this, the boy simply slapped her back. During that time Clarissa imagined herself as a young heroine alone in a hostile world. Apparently she believed that every situation had something to do with her, although very few did.

This tendency of Clarissa's might have developed further under different circumstances, but it so happened that only six months after she finished school, her life changed. During Christmas vacation in a provincial town, she met and married a local resident, and returned home in the role of a wife with an absentee husband. One cannot testify to her emotional transformation during this time; externally, however, she changed from a young person under attack from a hostile world into a silly young female who gives no thought to her circumstances and just goes along blindly. Physically, she changed too. The clumsy girl with glasses became a curvy beauty with golden hair and exquisite hands. As should have been expected, this soft and feminine Clarissa grew tired of her long-distance marriage with its numerous obligations, and when asked about her husband she would say she had no idea and felt tired of it all.

The next marriage followed quickly—to an ambulance doctor, a large man with thick arms. Soon after the birth of their child, Clarissa's husband began to drink, to see other women, and to beat her. Clarissa seemed unable to stop arguing with him, even when he wasn't around. At the office or when visiting a friend, she carried on her monologue in the same ringing note of protest, punctuated by sobs. Her husband's indifference and contempt caught her off guard: she didn't have a chance to regroup, to get used to her new role and think calmly about the best solution to her predicament. Even the youthful approach of dealing slaps for insults (remember the fight with her classmate) had abandoned her. One could say that during this period Clarissa moved like an amoeba, without direction, her goal simply to dodge the blows of her husband, who didn't restrain himself in anything and continued to behave like a rowdy animal in the same room with Clarissa and their baby.

The heaviest blow came when the husband left Clarissa and took the child to live with his parents. Clarissa threw herself again and again at the locked door of his parents' apartment—uselessly, it turned out, because they had rented a dacha somewhere in the country and had gone there with the boy, or so the neighbor informed Clarissa.

Clarissa's subsequent behavior could be described only as illogical and pointless. Every week-end she took the commuter rail in a random direction and roamed the countryside trying to spot her son's yellow hat. She called her husband's friends and colleagues, busy people with serious jobs, to ask them to help her kidnap her son. The only outcome of these actions was a visit from a doctor and a nurse who wanted to know how she slept and whether she was followed by secret enemies, and who mentioned the possibility of a free stay in a wonderful sanatorium where she'd be allowed to sleep as late as she wanted—for a whole week! Clarissa pointed out that no one would give her sick leave just to sleep, but the doctor assured her it would be easy and she didn't have to worry. "I see," said Clarissa. "He sent you. I understand." The doctor and nurse again tried to convince Clarissa to come with them, but Clarissa wasn't listening. She was sitting at the kitchen table deep in thought, with burning cheeks.

After this Clarissa disappeared from sight, and no one knows just how she resurfaced six months later in yet another role of divorced mother with child support for her small son and the perennial problem of child care.

In this role Clarissa proved to be no better or worse than thousands of other women, but she did exhibit a certain practical intelligence. For example, she didn't plan her future life with the boy. Any such plan was futile because the boy was extremely attached to his father and grandparents, who lavished him with care and comfort that Clarissa alone couldn't provide. So she focused on the pressing problems that encroached from every side. She calculated, to the second, the time it took to travel from her son's kindergarten to her work, spent her lunch break shopping for groceries, and treated her work duties as secondary, which was understandable for someone in her position.

After a year of this drudgery, she took a vacation by the Black Sea. She was there alone, her son at a summer camp with his kindergarten. For the first two weeks Clarissa couldn't let go of her motherly worries, and she ignored the sea, the sun, and the abundant southern fruit, thinking only of her son, whom she'd left in the rainy north. She spent hours at the post office, waiting to place a long-distance call to the kindergarten to find out if her boy was well and if he was still there. But eventually the sea, the sun, and the fruit worked their magic, and Clarissa experienced a second metamorphosis. A ripe woman of twenty-five, looking meek and detached behind her glasses, she was noticed (and deeply admired) by a certain airline pilot, Valery, who was spending a few hours at the beach between flights. That day he didn't dare approach Clarissa, because he was wearing underwear instead of swimming trunks. Instead he watched from a respectful distance while she rummaged nearsightedly through her purse, finally pulling out a touchingly small handkerchief to wipe her glasses with. Two days later Valery was again at the beach, this time properly attired. He positioned himself closer to Clarissa, but she was so frightened and repulsed by his attentions that she fled the beach hours before her usual time. The next day things improved a little, and Clarissa was able to squeeze out a few sentences. Afterward, she felt an enormous guilt and spent an entire day waiting at the post office to call her son's kindergarten. The boy was well; it hadn't rained.

Three months later Clarissa moved into Valery's spacious apartment. In time her son went to school, a girl was born, and one could say that life had finally stabilized for Clarissa and even begun to flow toward a peaceful, healthy maturity with its rotation of summer vacations, children's illnesses, and major purchases. On the days when Valery was on duty, Clarissa would call the airport dispatcher, demanding again and again Valery's flight information, and upon his return Valery would be forced to listen to reprimands for his wife's inappropriate behavior. Other than that, nothing clouded Clarissa and Valery's horizons.

Tamara's Baby

He never came by invitation—he never received one. He simply announced himself (often with a lengthy insult) through the door, then pleaded his way inside. At the dinner table he yelled and pontificated, spat out his food and bared his only tooth, wishing both to stuff himself and to have his say. He spoke in non sequiturs, always in a terrible hurry, never explaining anything. He must have believed it was the prerogative of an erudite man like himself to speak any way he wanted; didn't he spend all his unfilled and unpaid days in reading rooms, working on some obscure bibliography or biography? Just wait till it's done, he predicted to his poor hosts and their guests; he'd throw in some dirty laundry, some famous names, and voilà—we'd have a bestseller on our hands. But first he needed to finish this magnum opus with the help, he said, of foreign grants and lecture fees that never materialized. In the meantime, he lectured gratis in the smoking rooms of public libraries, where he showed up empty-handed, with no tobacco or matches of his own. Hence, the awkward giggling and convoluted openings—"God has nothing to do with religion" or "All politicians want is to be reelected; may I bother you for a smoke?"

The people who knew him feared he might ask to stay the night; women of the house shared the expression, "I could sense he was on the verge of staying over." Besides, he was old. (That didn't stop him from announcing into someone's intercom, "Let me in; it's up!") When he stayed, everything needed to be washed, aired, and dry-cleaned. Officially he was not homeless: after the divorce he was assigned an attic room with a ruined ceiling and exposed plumbing—imagine the smell. All he could do after the divorce was read, so he found refuge in public libraries, where he drank tap water and cadged leftovers from the cafeteria. Abandoned by his wife and children, he longed for hot food. On pension days his biggest splurge was a hot dog and sometimes one or even two hamburgers. Also on those days he'd call on his acquaintances, under the pretext of paying back a debt—thereby giving them reason to have him stay for dinner. The next day he'd be broke again and would go back to the same houses for another loan, or wait outside people's offices, ambushing them with requests for money to buy medicine.

That's how he lived for a long time, but things do change for someone like A.A., too. A fellow demagogue from the smoking room advised him about free health resort packages for the poor, and even helped him fill out an application at the office of social aid. That was over a year ago. Finally A.A. overheard someone bragging about going to a health resort for free. Ready to fight for his rights, he rushed to the social aid office and was informed that his request had been granted and that he had been expected at the resort two days ago. The woman at the counter blinked cleverly. He understood they were sending him in the off-season, in the worst weather, when no paying customer would go. He screamed and stomped his feet, but once outside he reconsidered. October wasn't so bad. Pushkin liked October. And if you think about it, what is a health resort? Three meals a day, plus he could take extra bread to keep him full at night. At the thought of all that food, he began to salivate uncontrollably. He

ran back to the library cafeteria to look for a leftover
piece of bread.

First stop: his old flophouse, the scene of many
battles. He spent the night there. In the morning he
exchanged his smelly rags for some decent secondhand clothing. Then he raided local Dumpsters for
a discarded suitcase and found one, in imitation
leather. He already owned a hat—a knit beret. He
tricked the attendant at the library cloakroom for a
scarf. "I must have left it here and then forgot. . . .
You see, I don't have a woman to look after me, so
things get lost. . . ." The woman picked out a green
rag that someone must have left ages ago and held
it out with disgust. "This one yours? Was about to
throw it out." A.A. accepted the rag gratefully and
scurried around the corner to try it on. The green
scarf went nicely with his new dark jacket and black
beret. Then the shoes: his smoking room buddies
suggested he look through the Dumpsters near big
department stores, as a lot of people tossed their
old shoes there after buying new ones. A.A. found a
decent-looking pair, a little too big, but that was
even better. In the evening he packed his notes and a
pen (cadged from the post office) into the suitcase.
There were eight days remaining at the health resort
and two weeks before his pension.

At dawn A.A. left his vile room and boarded

the train without a ticket. For the entire trip he stood next to the exit, shaking from fear and cold. Arriving at the resort, he found everything still closed. He dozed in the lobby, sitting up, like a gentleman, until the cafeteria opened for breakfast. Once it did, he stuffed himself with kasha and bread, swallowed three cups of sweet tea, and then stormed the little library. Straight as a rod, with his pen and writing paper in hand and his green scarf draped over one shoulder, he began by loudly demanding works by Spengler and Kierkegaard from the cute librarian. She shrugged her plump shoulders and sent him to the mystery section. A.A. yelled louder: The library needed more books, and he happened to know a certain warehouse where publishers dumped unsold copies. Just give him a truck and he'll bring back hundreds of books! The librarian seemed indifferent to the news: she didn't have a truck, and besides, people on vacation wanted light reading, like mysteries and detective stories.

At this point an elderly lady interfered. She overheard A.A. bragging and asked to take down the address of that mythical warehouse. As for the library, she agreed: they needed more serious books for the patrons like Professor (meaning him) and a PhD like herself. Well, almost—her thesis was finished, it was waiting in her desk, and she needed only to defend it.

"Me too," A.A. agreed eagerly. "Mine's also on my desk"—even though he had no desk. The cute librarian was forgotten; the educated pair was loudly discussing matters of cultural importance. Leaving the library, A.A. held the door for the lady, sweeping her off her feet with such chivalry.

They walked into the park, inhaling the smell of damp leaves and wood smoke, and sat down on a bench under an ancient tree. "To walk the blessed path," A.A. pontificated, "one must give up his possessions—only then can one reach the sacred door; but what happens if one doesn't own anything? Will the door open for him?" She listened to his blabbering, taking it in gratefully. They almost missed lunch. Again he gobbled down his portion and all the bread on the table; he asked the server if he could move to Tamara Leonardovna's table, but apparently there was no room. Ready for another walk, he waited impatiently for her to finish, but the lady excused herself—she needed rest. A.A. went to his room, too, and stretched out on the clean sheets, almost crying with joy.

After dinner A.A. stuffed his pockets with bread, and together they walked over to the stream. Again she listened meekly; this time he expanded on Francis of Assisi, who had walked the blessed path and considered every insult God's gift. Back in his room he made a mess of his squashed bread slices, to his roommate's displeasure. A.A. headed off the impending confrontation by running out into the hall, where people were watching television. He flopped on a couch and proceeded to watch one program after the next, annoying everyone with vitriolic comments and wild laughter.

Unforgettable days rolled by. The happy couple took walks in plain view, ignoring giggles. A.A. successfully campaigned for a transfer to Tamara Leonardovna's table—he simply moved there, and one of the enraged ladies switched tables in protest. What really bothered the others was Tamara's age (which they found out from the director's secretary). She was seventy-five—fourteen years older than he was! It was practically statutory rape, the resort ladies decided. Eventually public opinion ruled that this A.A. was simply looking for a perch, for someone—anyone—to take him in; for what kind of prince charming was he—without hair, teeth, or a roof over his head? Somehow they knew everything about him. A.A. couldn't keep his voice down to save his life. But Tamara didn't want to know. When, a week after they left the resort, one of the ladies called to check in on Tamara at home, A.A. picked up the phone. Like small children they were unable to part.

———

Now they are living together in Tamara's little apartment, away from prying eyes. A.A. eats regularly, before and after visiting the library. Tamara keeps house, looks after him, complains often but receives no sympathy; the blessed path is thorny. A.A. now owns two writing pads, which Tamara has purchased for him. She wants to have his pension recalculated and to make sure he receives benefits like a free subway pass—he used to beg and fake injuries to be let in.

Tamara's whole family is up in arms about this cohabitation, especially her nephews, who are terrified that the old fools may marry. They cannot deny, though, that Tamara looks fresher, or that she is full of plans and new energy. For example, she has located that mythical book warehouse and now takes books to nursing homes and hospitals, where people cannot afford them.

At night they squawk to each other about their day. Tamara complains and recites her grievances, and A.A. doles out advice and admonitions like an austere paterfamilias. Then they go to their beds and read, exchanging notes; in the morning they resume their squawking and arguing. Who knows why this

A.A. screams so much—he may be scared of losing her, of finding himself back in the flooded attic.

She refuses to marry him, although she did once kiss his hand when he was prostrate with illness. At night A.A. cries and howls with grief, but in the morning he plays boss again, and Tamara, barely awake, hurries with his eggs. He continues to show up uninvited at people's houses, but now he holds himself more assertively and makes frequent allusions to his wife, "so-called Tamara," and her undefended thesis on Charles Dickens.

Eggs is the luxury that graces their breakfast table the first three days after pension, but A.A. is shaved and dressed in everything clean, and Tamara walks around in practically new winter boots that A.A. fished out from a Dumpster. A.A. often criticizes her appearance: "So-called Tamara, go fix your hair!" Tamara crawls around her little apartment, always thinking about the next meal for this parasite. Where did he come from, helpless like all parasites and parasitic like all helpless people? And yet he criticizes and instructs, while she has no strength left to look after him. At the end of the day she drags herself to the food market to pick up from the floor squashed veggies and fruit for his dinner. She feels ashamed in the presence of some imaginary friends and nemeses, but she does have a justification: a certain old photo, the holiest of her secrets.

In the evening he comes home, gobbles down her vegetable stew in a second, and starts flailing his arms again, this time thrashing the very personage whose bibliography or biography he's been putting together for ten years. The man was a fraud, it turns out, and Tamara says, "I told you so," and they squawk some more and then watch television, exchanging acerbic comments.

That night he cannot stay asleep. He wakes up in tears. Tamara Leonardovna tucks him in and blows on his bald forehead, as she would have done for her baby if he had lived. And now for Tamara's secret: she never believed the baby had died at birth! No, you see, here was her son, with an altered date of birth; he was back to sleep. There is a photo of *him*, the baby's father, that she once thought she'd destroyed. It turned up mysteriously in the folder with her yellowing thesis. It's the same face as A.A.'s, only younger.

She holds out the photo with a trembling hand, but he pushes it away: "What does that have to do with me? What's wrong with you? Look at the date: I wasn't even born yet." He goes back to watching their tiny old television, and she puts away the photo, wanting to say to him, "My little one."

A Happy Ending

———

Young Berries

A mother brought her girl to a sanatorium for sickly children and then left. I was that girl.

The sanatorium overlooked a large pond encircled by an autumnal park, with meadows and paths. The tall trees seemed ablaze with gold and copper; the scent of their falling leaves made the girl dizzy, after the city's stench. Once upon a time, the sanatorium was a gentleman's stately manor, with classical pillars, arched ceilings, and upper galleries. The girls' dormitory, called a *dortoir*, was once a drawing room with a grand piano.

The revolution had repurposed the estate into

a sanatorium and school for proletarian children with tuberculosis. By the time the girl reached fifth grade, of course, all Soviet citizens were proletarians. They lived in crowded, communal apartments, traveled in streetcars packed with commuters, waited in lines for seats in public cafeterias, and so on. (They waited also for bread, potatoes, shoes, and, on rare occasions, a luxury like a winter coat; in communal apartments, workers stood in line to use the bathroom.) A well-regulated line represented fairness. One had only to wait long enough for one's portion, as, indeed, the girl had waited for her spot at the Forest School—that was the name of the sanatorium.

I cannot describe the girl's appearance. Appearances cannot reveal inner life, and the girl, who was twelve at the time, carried on a continuous inner monologue, deciding every second—what to say, where to sit, how to answer—with the single purpose of behaving exactly like the other children, to avoid being kicked and shunned. But the girl wasn't strong enough to control her every step, to be at all times a model of neatness and moderation. She wasn't strong enough, so she would run through the rainy autumnal park in torn stockings, her mouth flapping open in an excited yelp, simply because, you see, they were playing hide-and-seek. Between classes she'd stampede the hallways, snot-nosed, hair undone, fighting and cawing, what a sight.

The sanatorium expected all students to keep track of their basic belongings. One week into the school term, no one, including the girl, could locate his or her own pens, pencils, erasers. But the girl lost her handkerchief, too, followed by her right mitten, her scarf, and one of her two stockings. (One lies there by the bed; the other, God knows where.) Plus, she was missing one of her rubber boots! Without her boots, she could neither walk through the park's muddy puddles nor enter the dining hall. In an old boot from her teacher, she dragged herself like a pariah behind everyone in class.

Such was my condition at the very moment I needed to look no worse than the others. There was this boy, Tolik. We were the same age, but he was six inches shorter, and unspeakably beautiful: a chiseled nose surrounded by freckles, thick lashes over starry eyes, his mouth poised for a coy smirk. The girl was too tall for him, but this young god radiated his charm evenly and meaninglessly a hundred yards around like a little nuclear reactor. When he entered the dining hall, the space around his table lit up, and the girl felt a surge of merriment—Tolik's here!— and Tolik's eyes would grow larger, as though under a magnifying glass, as he surveyed his kingdom.

Heads turned toward him like sunflowers to the sun. The girl felt stabbed in her heart. There was a swelling right above it, the size of a young berry.

In a commune, no one is entitled to private meals; that's considered hoarding. Everything, even poor biscuits from home, must be shared. A commune also dislikes nonconforming behavior, such as arriving late or wearing mismatched boots. The girl, inevitably, became an outcast in her class. She began to straggle behind on purpose to avoid scornful looks. One October night, at the end of her second week, she fell so far behind the other girls that she found herself alone among the boys. Dark shadows fell across the path, cutting her off from the girls and their teacher up ahead. The boys, like a pack of wolves encircling its prey, surrounded her.

The girl stood there on the edge of the park. The other girls, protected and safe, she could barely see.

I screamed after them. I bellowed like a tuba, like a siren.

The boys nearest to me grinned stupidly. (Later, in my grown life, I could always recognize that dumb smirk, a companion to base, dirty deeds.) Their arms opened wide, ready to grab me. Their fingers danced, and their berries probably hardened. I stood still, screaming toward the girls. A few glanced back, but they all continued to walk away, even faster. I screamed louder.

What would they do to me?

They'd have to tear me to pieces and bury my remains, but before that, they would do everything that could be done to a person who becomes their property.

For now, they just wanted me to shut up.

When they were only five feet away, something made them pause. I hurled myself through their ring and ran wildly across the meadow, losing my over-size boot in the mud. At the door, I overtook the last of the girls. She heard me thumping and looked around: on her face I saw the same dirty, complicit smirk. I tumbled inside, red and swollen from crying. But nobody asked a single question as to what caused all that yelling in the park. Those girls knew instinctively. Maybe they'd shared a past in the caves where their female ancestors had been chased down and raped. (How quickly children can regress and accept such hard, primitive truths! Fire and women to be used in common; collective meals shared equally—where the strong get more, the weak get less or nothing at all; sleep together on a filthy floor; grab food from the pile; dress in identical rags.)

That night the girls seemed quiet in a strange,

contented way, as if their hunger for primitive justice had been stoked and sated. They didn't know I
had escaped! They assumed I had come back alive
but broken, soiled.

Excreted was the word for such children. The
girl herself had known excreted kids in her school-
yard. The excreted were outside the commune, up
for grabs—anyone could abuse them in any way.
The thing to do was to stalk them, then to slam them
into a wall in plain view. The excreted wore the look
of dumb cattle; two or three stalkers tailed them.
Nothing less than constant adult supervision could
protect them, but one can't expect an adult presence
on every path, or around each corner.

The next day began like any other. I fished my
boot out of the mud. The boys greeted me as usual
(slugging me on the neck, shoving me into a puddle)
while the girls watched me like hawks. But no one
hollered, no one pointed fingers—eventually it became clear that nothing truly awful had happened to
me. I must have escaped. Life returned to normal.

One person at the sanatorium, Tolik, sensed that
something had happened. Tolik, a prime chaser, possessed the sharpest hunter's instincts in the pack. He
began stalking me. In dark corners, his starry eyes
searched my body while his cohort guarded the pe-
rimeter glumly—this chase wasn't theirs. It wasn't a

courtship, exactly; it was something else, something the girls couldn't find a name for. They shrugged their shoulders. I alone understood that Tolik was drawn to the whiff of shame that clung to me.

The girl was left alone. She'd won her place in the sun, with her powerful lungs and her refusal to cave in. It turned out she was blessed with an exceptionally strong voice (she could bellow as low as a hippo and screech as high as a drunken cat), and this talent could kick in at a moment's danger. In addition, she'd pushed herself academically, and this, too, mattered at Forest School, which wasn't just any public summer camp where a child was measured by her ability to wake up on time. Good grades were considered an honest achievement here—you couldn't get an A by punching noses—so if a teacher read your composition in front of the class, then that was hard to sneer at.

I'd spent my childhood in lines at public cafeterias and in the kitchen of our communal apartment, where academic excellence didn't matter to my survival. Now, pitted against this hostile tribe, I applied myself feverishly to writing a composition about autumn. My final draft piled azure skies upon turquoise dusk, bronze upon gold, and crystals upon corals, and the astonished teacher—a consumptive beauty in an orthopedic corset—passed my opus around to the other teachers and then read it aloud to the entire class—the same class that had nearly destroyed me.

I followed up with some verse for a special edition, in honor of Constitution Day, of the school's newspaper. It wasn't real poetry, the kind that spills out of a dying person like blood and becomes the butt of ruthless jokes. No, my creation was beyond mockery; it could bring only respect. The Soviet people are the strongest in the world, I wrote, and they want peace for every nation—six lines in all. "Your own work?" the beautiful teacher asked as her corset squeaked.

A new pair of rubber boots arrived from home. At night, in the electric light of the girls' latrine, I memorized spelling rules. My powerful new voice was now part of the school choir, and I was chosen to dance, too, in a swift Moldavian circle dance—the school was preparing the New Year's program. After this, we would all go home.

That meant I would never again see my tormentor, my Tolik—your name like sweet, warm milk; your face shining over me like the sun; your eyes alive with indolence and lust.

In dark corners, Tolik showered me with obscenities. Six inches shorter but straight and unwavering as an arrow, he was a high-strung, consumptive boy keen on his target. Everyone at school grew used to the sight of the tall girl pushed against the wall, trapped between Tolik's arms. Every night I dreamed of his face.

The girl pulled on her new boots and trudged through the snowy park to meet her mother—her time in paradise was up; she was going home. At the winter palace, among crystals and corals of frozen trees, Tolik was living the final hours of his reign.

At the New Year's concert I performed solo in front of the choir, then swirled in a wild Moldavian dance. (For you alone, my Tolik.) Tolik performed, too (it turned out he possessed a beautifully clear soprano), singing of Soviet Motherland and her brave sons, the aviators, to the accompaniment of a grand piano. He was visibly nervous. The absence of his cynical smirk so struck his classmates that they clapped uncertainly, surprised at their king's need for their approval.

After the concert there was a dinner, followed by a formal dance. In the early 1950s, children still were taught the orderly dances of the aristocratic finishing schools—polonaise, pas de quatre, pas d'Espagne—and so a slow minuet was announced, ladies ask gentlemen. Tolik, recovered from his stage fright, was exchanging smirks with his entourage. I walked over to him. Our icy fingers entwined. We

curtsied and bowed woodenly across the floor. Tolik, discomfited to see me sniffling in public, didn't
crack jokes. Instead, after the dance, he respect-
fully walked me over to my nook behind a pillar. I
retired to the *dortoir* and wept there until the girls
returned. There were no more heady interrogations
in dark corners. Tolik didn't know what to do with
me anymore.

I was picked up last, as always. We walked along
the white highway, under dark skies, dragging my
poor suitcase. The *dortoir* windows were throwing
farewell lights on the snowy road.

I never saw Tolik again, but I heard his sil-
very voice over the phone. He called me at home, in
Moscow.

My grandfather's daughter from his second
marriage occupied the next room in our communal
apartment. She yelled for me to come to the phone.
"For you," she announced with her usual bug-eyed
look. "Some guy."

"What guy? There's no guy. . . . Hello?"

"It's Tolik, remember?" the high voice sang out.

"Oh, it's you, Lena," I greeted Tolik, with a significant glance at my aunt and my mother, who'd
also come into the hall. "It's Lena Mitiaieva from
school, Mom."

The unmarried Uncle Misha, a radiologist at the

KGB clinic, decided to join the party. He stood in his blue army long johns between the black draperies of his doorway. The apartment's entire population now stood in the hall (minus the Kalinovskys, minus my grandfather's second wife, minus the grandfather who was smoking shag tobacco in bed, minus the janitor, Aunt Katya). The conceit was that everyone was waiting to use the phone after me.

"It's me, Tolik," continued the voice.

"No, Lena, I can't tonight—they are going to the movies, Mom," an aside to my mother.

"What movies? It's late," my mother answered quickly, while Uncle Misha and my aunt seemed to be waiting for more.

My love, my holiest secret, was calling me! And I had to speak to him in front of everyone!

"No, Lena, why?" I kept repeating vaguely, because Tolik was inviting me to join him right away at the Grand Illusion for a movie. Swooning, I kept mumbling nonsense for my listeners' benefit. The listeners guessed the truth. They wanted to see me squirm.

Azure skies, turquoise dusk, minuet, my tears, his icy fingers all vanished, and remained in paradise. Here was another story—here I was a fifth-grader with a chronic cold and torn brown stockings. The world of crystals and corals, of miraculous deliveries, of undying love—that world couldn't coexist with the communal apartment and my grandfather's room in particular, full of books and bedbugs, where my mother and I (officially homeless) were allowed to sleep in a corner under his desk. My Tolik, my little prince, my dauphin, couldn't possibly be standing in a dark stinking phone booth near the grimy Grand Illusion.

I didn't believe Tolik, and rightly so, for I could hear coarse voices in the background and hoots of laughter. Again, the tightening circle of dirty smirks. But this time I was far away.

"Neighbors want the phone," I concluded indifferently (choking back tears). "Bye, Lena."

Tolik called again after that, inviting me to go skating or to see a movie. "No, Lena, why?" I mumbled. "What do you mean, 'Why?'" giggled the shameless Tolik.

Tolik, that prime chaser, had figured out how to use my unhappy love for his dark purposes. But— the circle of animal faces had never crushed the girl; the terror remained among the tall trees of the park, in the enchanted kingdom of young berries.

The Adventures of Vera

Vera turned sixteen, and nothing but scenes followed, one after the next. Her father begged her to have some self-respect, not to fall to pieces over every stranger. He even threatened to send her to a juvenile facility but, in the end, didn't act soon enough. When Vera was twelve, her teachers observed that her mental development lagged behind her extraordinary physical maturity; one of them, who respected Vera's father, told him she couldn't imagine what would happen to Vera when she turned fourteen. But Vera did turn fourteen, and fifteen. At sixteen she quit school, without asking anyone, and apprenticed herself as a junior salesgirl at a department store. Vera's coworkers haloed her with gentle understanding and slightly patronizing friendship, agreeing that she wasn't all there.

Often they said to her, "Greetings from Ivan the Fool!" They were referring, of course, to love, for what else could girls of eighteen talk about? They discussed other things, naturally: books, weather, terrible accidents in the city, injustice and deceit, their childhoods, the constant ache in their feet, and problems at work. But mostly they spoke about friendship and love, tried to analyze their feelings, applied intuition or simply closed their eyes to everything and cried their hearts out, and gradually, in the course of those conversations, acquired a protective layer of hardness that sealed their mouths and left them to fight their grown-up battles alone, wordlessly.

Vera's father didn't understand the benefits of such friendship, considering it unhealthy for Vera. When Vera announced that she was ready to leave the store, he agreed, despite misgivings, to arrange a position for her at his institute. The father was understandably afraid that after four years behind a sales counter, in a corrupting atmosphere of intimate women's talk, Vera might go a little cuckoo from the institute's abundance of men, might be willing to bestow her trust on any man—any man, of course, other than him.

Barely a month after Vera started at the institute, her father was informed that Vera's coworkers found her behavior odd to the point of indecency. She carried on long conversations over the office phone, wore too much makeup, giggled loudly, and, in general, behaved as if she were at a party rather than a place of work. The first thing she did, her father was informed, was type a personal letter, on the office typewriter, to a certain Mr. Drach. Vera thanked Mr. Drach for returning five rubles and apologized for not agreeing to disclose her friend Tatiana's address without her permission. Vera's father considered the dates in question and decided, with no small relief, that the letter to Mr. Drach must have referred to details about Vera's recent vacation at a country resort, and did not represent a new crisis.

Soon enough, however, he learned that Vera was pursuing an employee in her department, a married man who had invited her for a car ride one night but the next day avoided her and then had to ask a coworker to tell her quietly, "Now's not the time." Yet Vera continued to follow him around, demanding an explanation! She moped over this aborted romance, as she thought of it, for weeks. She couldn't have known that the man's wife, a former ballerina, had found out about their little excursion and made a horrible scene. No one told Vera anything, including her father, who felt determined to have a little talk with her but, as before, couldn't work up the nerve.

While he hesitated, another employee, a rising star in Vera's department, asked Vera to stay late to take dictation. About this young man, it was known he had recently filed for divorce, on the grounds of childlessness, and that he lived alone, without his parents, in a condo in the suburbs. The next morning Vera returned to the office convinced she had experienced a life-changing romantic event—she had found the love of her life, a future husband. She cast mysterious looks around the office, and trembled with anticipation. This employee, however, behaved exactly like the first one, as if Vera reminded him of something unpleasant that he wanted to forget. When one of his colleagues, a woman, mentioned to him that Vera was crying and was ready to quit the institute, he told her (the exact quote was reported to Vera's father), "Let Vera bring me a doctor's note saying she's healthy; then I'll do it." He said this in front of everyone. They all laughed. Again, poor Vera didn't have a clue. Imagining that someone had informed him of her unfortunate car ride, she hung out in the corridors and halls, looking for a chance to reassure him—nothing had happened that night in the car, none of it was her fault, nothing was ever her fault, and so on. Vera would have dumped her entire biography on the poor fellow—or anyone else, if they had cared to listen.

Her father was absolutely determined to open Vera's eyes to the reality of the situation, to clarify the circumstances and motives. But he was afraid of Vera's reaction, and besides, none of his past explanations had done much good. For a long time after her disappointment, Vera performed her duties automatically, ate very little, went to bed early, and read a lot of poetry. To her friends she admitted she had lost interest in living. She felt like an old woman.

Between this disaster and the final, decisive romance from that period of Vera's life, there was a brief friendship with another one of her coworkers, a man of very short stature who always winked and smiled at Vera, and called her Miss, and tried to steal a kiss when no one was looking. This man, who was known in their department for his prim manners, entertained Vera with sexual anecdotes and once brought her an illustrated volume on the subject. Sitting on top of her desk in her little nook, he relaxed, cursing out everyone in the department and making personal phone calls that made Vera blush. All this, too, ended on an odd note, but not before

Vera became fond of his visits and learned to think of him as a close friend.

When the man asked Vera to help him buy a warm coat (it was impossible to get one off the rack in his size), Vera raised a flurry of activity among her friends in retail, and arranged for him to pick up a fine, imported coat in a certain store, at a certain time. On the day of the appointment, the little employee didn't come to work. Vera called his office number all day at regular intervals, announcing in the same flat, official voice that it was Ms. Vera calling about the coat. At first her calls were answered with muffled laughter, then simply ignored. The next day the little employee read Vera a forceful lecture on the subject of appropriate behavior in the workplace, after which he stopped what he called Vera's "education"—the jokes, sitting on her desk, and so on.

This insignificant episode shook Vera to her core. She felt she'd been abandoned by a fiancé, whom she had come to like and even find attractive, despite his obvious shortcomings. Her father received a full description of the incident: how the little employee's officemates doubled up with laughter during Vera's calls; how the next day they all congratulated him on becoming the latest victim of Vera's prowess; and how, on hearing about this, the married employee with the car talked about Vera with disgust and almost malice, while the department's rising star also made ironic comments, although not as harsh, restraining himself out of respect for his female colleagues. Nothing the little employee could say about his real need for a coat stopped the giggling; finally, he gave up and, when no women were present, made a remark so dirty that his audience choked with laughter.

Vera fell in love with the head of her department when he returned from an overseas business trip and asked her to type up his report. All through the dictation he interspersed amusing little comments about the trip and its participants, as if only Vera with her superior taste and understanding deserved to know the real facts. Vera was smitten. Never before had she been addressed by a superior with such complete trust, as an equal. She didn't consider, of course, that her boss simply wanted to deploy his charm on a new employee, or that, like most men in his position, he needed from time to time to feel the spontaneous adulation of the lowest ranks. Isolated in her nook, barred from general staff meetings, Vera wasn't aware of the atmosphere of jealousy and of love for the boss (absolutely platonic) that permeated the entire department; nor was she familiar with his notorious habit of alternating charm with outbursts of the deepest cynicism in his personal relationships with his employees. During the next dictation, the boss grew even more relaxed and had a playful argument with Vera about some movie whose name they couldn't remember. The loser had to fulfill a wish; Vera lost. With a mix of anxiety, regret, and bubbling joy, she prepared to give all of herself to the man she loved. But the boss didn't ask for anything like that. Instead, he quickly wrapped up his report, grabbed his briefcase from his office, and practically ran home.

Over the next few weeks, Vera waited for a phone call or a note. After another sleepless night she called his office from a pay phone and asked for an appointment. This in itself was a strange request—employees at Vera's department dropped in on their boss at any time, without formalities. The boss agreed, however. He told Vera to come by at the end of the day and to knock slowly on his door three times. Vera showed up at the appointed time and stayed for more than an hour, talking and talking about herself, as if a dam had burst. The boss listened with interest, saying now and again, "Fascinating" and "I'm going to study you." At the end of her monologue, he agreed to meet her for a date later that night, adding that they must leave the building separately, in case someone might see them and think God knows what.

As her father might have warned her, Vera waited for ninety minutes at some tram stop, in the cold, in a remote blue-collar neighborhood where her boss must have spent his factory youth. Luckily, she had another date planned for later that night, and also luckily, that young man waited patiently for her. Vera's evening wasn't entirely wasted.

Eros's Way

At work her nickname was Pulcheria, after the meek and faithful wife in Gogol's famous story. Pulcheria was a model spouse by nature, but that hadn't stopped her husband from making a certain acquaintance at a vacation resort, after which came anonymous phone calls and threats that the lady would "take gas." The closing act was the appearance of a mutilated photograph of Pulcheria outside her door. In the epilogue Pulcheria was left alone, raising two daughters.

When her younger daughter married, Pulcheria aged rapidly, almost willingly, her lovely eyes and innocent soul withdrawing beneath heavy flesh, seemingly forever. Her soul still flickered on occasion—at work, for instance, where she cared deeply about her little subject. She fell ill when a new boss swooped into their division like an evil genius, threatening to ruin years of painstaking research. That was when Pulcheria and her colleague, Olga, formed a strategic alliance and became friends.

This Olga, for whom work was her life, hated their new boss with a special intensity. At home, people said, Olga had a sick husband who was hospitalized routinely, and, they added, her only son had married an older woman, had a baby with her, and now demanded one-third of the parental apartment. Olga fought ferociously. In the end the young family settled into a tiny room in the woman's parents' house. Olga lost her rosy complexion but remained in her palace, with her sick husband.

One evening Pulcheria stayed late at the office— earlier in the day she had been invited unexpectedly to Olga's house for a birthday party. She called her daughter (who lived with Pulcheria) to give her instructions for the night but continued to worry about her and the baby; in retrospect this seems almost funny because only a day later she would barely remember their faces or anything else from her previous life. Everything happened so fast; she seemed to have gone to sleep, or else to have lost her mind from shock, as her colleagues (Olga among them) believed. When she left the office, she began following in Eros's way—of which she hadn't the slightest awareness.

At the party Pulcheria wound her way into a dark corner and sat there quietly, while the hostess and her coiffed girlfriends set the table in the dining room (Pulcheria couldn't even count the rooms in that fabulous apartment). She understood Olga's motives for inviting her—she always understood people's true motives, to her discomfort. Olga simply wanted to crush Pulcheria with the glamour of her party, then oust their hateful new boss with Pulcheria's help (there were only three people in their division), and, finally, get herself appointed in the boss's place.

Pulcheria was angry with herself for wasting her whole evening on this party where everyone and everything felt alien and uninteresting to her. But she was angrier with their boss, who intended to turn their archives into a profit-making tabloid featuring personal letters and who-slept-with-whom exposés. The employees nicknamed the boss Tsarina and quickly figured out that she intended to write her doctoral thesis from their research. They also discovered that she'd been installed there by her husband, the deputy director at a sister research institute, who, in turn, found a position for their own director's nephew, an equally useless careerist. Knowing all this made them want to cry from shame and hopelessness—but what could they do?

That's why Pulcheria observed the surrounding luxury with indifference, using the party as simply a chance to take a break from the daily drudgery she suffered behind her perfect image of a plump, almost ancient grandmother—though Pulcheria was no more than two months older than youthful-looking Olga. Pulcheria recklessly played at old age at a time when quite a few women picked themselves up and stayed in shape for a long time. Olga, for instance, recently had made herself look even younger with the help of cosmetic surgery. Pulcheria felt a little scared of Olga's taut face and avoided looking directly at it, a habit Olga interpreted as an admission of inferiority. One could see through Olga at a glance, while Pulcheria was shielded by an ironic guardian angel who understood everything about everyone—which was why Pulcheria just sighed when their third colleague, the genuinely young Camilla, made some wisecracks about Olga's surgery. Incidentally, Camilla had not been invited to Olga's party. Olga had probably decided that in her war with the boss, Pulcheria was a safer bet than the rebellious Camilla, who, by the way, would not have wanted to waste an evening with old hags. She had other plans, dreams to pursue, so let's not worry about this Camilla—she didn't come to the institute from the street, either; she, too, had relatives in the right places.

After whiling away in her corner, Pulcheria joined the other guests at the dinner table and continued her inconspicuous existence. She nibbled and drank a little until she realized the guest on her right was asking her name. She told him, and they began to talk about a certain scholar whose life happened to be Pulcheria's special subject. The scholar had been exposed and denounced; these days his name was mentioned only pejoratively, but Pulcheria knew and loved him as an etymologist might love a bug she's discovered, even if it's harmful. In a quiet, reserved voice, Pulcheria firmly dismissed the pejorative note in her neighbor's tone. Her neighbor brought up some familiar arguments, but Pulcheria didn't want to debate a layman and just sighed. Only once did she bother to correct him, and her correction was so elegant and to the point that the guest looked at her intently as if seeing her for the first time. Pulcheria, too, focused her tired eyes and through her exhaustion saw a missing front tooth and blinking pale eyes; but what she really saw was an innocent, dreamy young boy.

The guest kept looking at Pulcheria and smiling. There are people who smile at everything and everyone, and one shouldn't take their smiles personally, but this man smiled with a purpose. He smiled in admiration of Pulcheria's intelligence, of her brilliant conversation, and as a result Pulcheria fell in love—a pitying, tender love.

She blossomed, her angelic soul delivering a ray of kindness, and thus the matter was settled. Quietly but firmly Pulcheria described her scholarly pursuits, but the subject of their conversation was of no importance; only the essence mattered, and the essence was that these two people had found each other at a noisy dinner table, while their hostess flew to the kitchen and back, beaming with purple blush on her new cheeks—although on one of her trips she did stop to whisper something loudly in the guest's ear. A loud whisper of this kind usually carries an insult for the person nearby, but Pulcheria understood nothing of what was said. When Olga left, their conversation resumed, and when Pulcheria got up to leave, the guest followed her to the door, changed out of his house slippers and into winter boots, and walked out with her. They walked to the metro station in the crisp, cold air, and somehow Pulcheria wasn't embarrassed by her coat with its hanging threads or her balding fur hat, which she'd been wearing since college. Her face shone; her eyes opened up; her guardian angel worked his way to the surface through the layers of aged flesh.

They walked down the steps to the train. He rode with her to her station, and then they walked again, for a long time, all the way to her door. There he kissed her hand, then left. They didn't exchange phone numbers. Pulcheria didn't even ask his name. She disappeared into the dark entrance, thinking of nothing, but later that night she woke up in despair, realizing she couldn't ask Olga anything about him, not even his name.

The next day Olga got into another scrape with their boss, who asked her to fetch a folder from the file cabinet, even though they were in the same room. A hissing exchange ensued, an exchange that Pulcheria, absorbed in her dreams about the Stranger, missed entirely. Olga seemed to avoid Pulcheria and didn't invite her to lunch, either sensing Pulcheria's new indifference or feeling indifferent herself. Nonetheless, Pulcheria brought her tray to Olga's table. In spite of her decision not to ask any questions, she immediately asked, "So how did it end?"

"What do you mean, how?"

"Well, I did leave early. . . ."

"Ah, who cares about washing dishes? But what do you think of her? Treating me like her secretary! And who is she? Just the wife of our idiot director's friend. And she thinks she can boss us around!"

Olga then made a short speech about her own connections, which she had, it turned out, at the highest level; and speaking of husbands, her own husband was still very much respected as a mathematician, despite his illness.

"What's wrong with him?" Pulcheria asked indifferently, still hoping to shift the conversation back to the party, to the Stranger.

"The worst," Olga announced. "Schizophrenia."

Pulcheria felt she had to say something comforting.

"I don't trust such diagnoses," she said calmly.

"He's had it for a long time, it turns out. He complained about his stomach, lost a lot of weight, quarreled at work, and then they didn't pass his thesis. . . ."

"But what's so crazy about it?" Pulcheria asked. "Dissertations don't make it through committees all the time!"

"At the hospital he was smashing his fist into the wall. They thought it was from some sort of pain, but then they asked me, and I told them everything. He was calling for you, they told me, for Anya."

"Anya?" Now Pulcheria was really listening: it was as though Olga were trying to tell her something. She didn't yet know that her entire future was outlined in this conversation.

"That's right—Anya. As if anyone ever wanted him except me. At least he doesn't have my office number; at my previous job he called ten times a day. A jealous nut."

"So how are you coping?" Pulcheria asked weakly.

"How? At least he's still okay in bed or else I'd hang myself, that's how. Did you notice the men at my party? My lovers—all of them. And their wives are my friends. So what shall we do about this bitch?"

Olga's story confronted Pulcheria with the shadowy, murky aspect of life where photographs get mutilated and then dropped on family doorsteps. These disturbing thoughts alternated with waves of misery. On the outside Pulcheria appeared to be processing the same old letter over and over. Later that evening, approaching her house with heavy grocery bags, she saw at the darkened entrance his uncovered gray head. Casually and simply he appeared before her. They walked to her apartment.

The young family's room was dark and quiet; either they were walking the baby, or all three were resting before the sleepless night, because the baby often cried between three and five in the morning. The kitchen was strewn with drying diapers. Pulcheria invited the guest into her neat little room, which was furnished with shabby but genuine antiques: her grandmother's little round table, and two bookcases with old books. The guest began looking through the books. Pulcheria brought some tea and fried potatoes; they ate in silence. The guest was absorbed in a book. He read a little longer, then got up to leave. They didn't touch. After he left, Pulcheria took the book from the table and pressed it to her breast.

Every night after work she flew home, skipping groceries. She cleaned, cooked, and scrubbed, barely understanding what she was doing. She couldn't eat, and lost a lot of weight. He came every night, always bringing the same pastry. They had tea, then he read to her or scribbled formulas. Her daughter and son-in-law quickly got used to the visitor and greeted him politely but didn't linger with conversation, so purposeful did he look, as did Pulcheria when she arrived home to greet him.

At work Pulcheria kept her nose to her desk. Olga lost interest in her. In a reverse move, Olga joined forces with Tsarina against young Camilla, who was always late or on sick leave but otherwise got her work done and indeed recently submitted a substantial article. Eventually it became clear that Camilla was expecting a baby and needed to keep her job until her maternity leave. Tsarina and Olga started a search for Camilla's replacement and interviewed candidates right in Camilla's presence. Poor Camilla tried to protest but continued to swell and barely dragged her feet. Clearly Olga and Tsarina needed a constant target for their warfare, and at least it was Camilla for now, but Pulcheria knew her turn would come eventually. A rumor spread through the institute that Pulcheria wasn't all there because she was late with her reports, never came to the cafeteria, and spent her lunch breaks buying groceries. But how could she write her reports if *he* sat in her room every night like a rock? She worked at night, and in the morning she dragged herself to work, where she scribbled meaninglessly on her index cards, barely awake.

After eight weeks of this, her mystery guest vanished. Three horrible days later Pulcheria forced herself to go to the cafeteria and to join Olga and Tsarina at their table. They were glad to see her and advised her to get a consultation with a good shrink (Olga offered her contacts). Tsarina praised Pulcheria's article, which was finally finished; Olga praised her thinness; and then the two resumed a conversation that almost made Pulcheria faint.

"So I won't be here till lunch," Olga announced meaningfully.

Tsarina replied that she could do as she wanted.

"Because, you see, he is in the ward for the violent, where he can easily be killed—the orderlies can do it. He needs to be transferred to the second floor, where they know him. Where he is now they'll make him a vegetable or an impotent."

Tsarina smacked her lips in sympathy.

"When I called the ambulance, he wouldn't go peacefully and screamed for help—that's why they put him with the violent."

Here Pulcheria asked whom they were talking about.

"My husband," Olga said. Her cheeks were ashy. "And guess what he yelled? That I was his enemy! He tried to push the window out with his head, cut himself, and then our cat ran in and began licking his blood like a cannibal. . . ."

"How did it all begin?" Pulcheria asked, barely breathing.

"The usual way: he started to disappear from home, then come back a day or two later, dirty and hungry. . . ."

She's lying, Pulcheria thought.

"What else. . . ?" Olga continued. "Couldn't sleep, didn't talk to anyone, went to work once a week; but you know what they think of him—a genius! He submits an article once a year, and the whole pack write their dissertations based on it. I went to talk to his boss, who promised to send him to a health spa. . . . Then he tried to jump. . . ." Tears were streaming down Olga's unlined face.

Now Pulcheria knew. She just needed to find out where they were keeping him.

"He'll be out," she promised. "My brother was at Kashchenko Asylum, and they let him out."

"Well, we haven't been to Kashchenko yet," Olga replied wistfully. "We go to the clinic that took him the very first time, when he was calling for Anya. He almost smashed a brick wall there with his fist."

Tsarina remarked that everything would be fine—they'd let him out, and things would resume their normal course.

"Maybe, maybe. . . . Still, how much can one take? Listen to this. . . ." And Olga related that "the bitch"—that is, her son's wife—wanted to sue Olga and her husband for housing—again!

"I keep telling that son of mine, 'Whatever you get through the courts will eventually be hers; she'll divorce you as soon as you have a place of your own!'"

It was the righteous rage of a person who fought a long and dirty battle to be alone in a huge apartment.

Pulcheria, petrified, listened attentively.

"The funny thing," Olga observed, returning to her husband, "is that he always finds some slut to look after him. They visit him at the hospital, bring him chicken soup. Thank God they don't let anyone in now because of the flu epidemic. Only letters. He refuses to eat anyway."

"Just like my brother," Pulcheria said. "But he was a political dissident, so they fed him through a tube."

"I don't know about dissidents," Olga replied irritably. "This one wouldn't eat because of schizophrenia; it's a form of self-cure—that's what the doctor said. On the floor for the violent, they don't fuck around, you know. The moment you stop eating they electroshock you: it feels like an electric chair, they say, only you get many jolts."

Pulcheria held herself together with her last reserves of strength; she knew Olga was waiting for her to squirm like a lab mouse. Finally the lunch ended, and Pulcheria could crawl back to her desk. Her suffering had ended and his begun, on the floor for the sick animals. From a woman rejected by her lover, Pulcheria had transformed into a woman

forcefully separated from him—an enormous differ-
ence. She even felt some small sympathy for Olga.
She was thinking calmly, resting after the horror of
the last three days. Waves of love rocked her over the
unwashed floor of her office, over dusty letters,
and she whispered words of affection, sending him
strength and support. Someday his suffering would
end, she told herself, but she must act with the ut-
most caution, calculate every step until the final victory, his freedom—although, as she knew from her
brother's experience, things were not so simple; and
getting the person out wasn't the end of it. The issue
of violated human rights was the easy, formal aspect
of the problem; the real problem was forcing the person off his perch, his customary place in life, even
when the place was such as his. One must never
force anyone; people must do everything themselves. Think of all those who tried to help him before, all those women with their chicken soup—where
are they now? They all vanished into oblivion, but
she, Pulcheria, must stay in his life, remain his loyal,
humble wife. She must wait. Victory would come.
What had been done to him was too fragrantly
unlawful—his son would get him out. Victory
would come, but without her. Oh pain of pains—not
to know anything! Not to see him!

"Would you like to come to the hospital with

me?" she heard Olga's voice over her shoulder. "After all, you were sitting next to him at the party; you talked to him all night, forgot about the rest of us."

"So that was your husband?" Pulcheria asked in an even tone.

"Of course it was. He took you home, didn't he? I asked him to."

"He walked me to the bus stop, that's all. How was I supposed to know he was ill? I'm afraid of mental patients; I don't even write to my brother in the U.S."

"Still, I wonder," Olga announced, staring at the dirty wallpaper above Pulcheria's desk. "I wonder where all these sluts come from—the ones who chase after sick people."

"Well, I haven't chased after anyone," Pulcheria objected coldly. "He invited himself. We only walked to the bus stop. I had no idea he was sick."

"Come with me, then. Tsarina will let us both go."

"I have a little grandson at home."

"But this is during work hours!"

"Why would I go there? I'm no one to him, a stranger."

"He won't yell at me so much in your presence."

"I'm afraid," Pulcheria said, and pulled out the next package of old letters.

"You didn't happen to see where he went after

he took you to the bus stop? Because all this time he's been living with someone; he hasn't slept with me, that much I know."

"Not my fault," Pulcheria responded coldly. "You should have heard what he said about my old man." Pulcheria pointed at the portrait of her scholar, the one in which he had a mustache like Hitler's and pince-nez like Beria's. "He said I'm wasting my time on the old bastard."

"Yes, that he does well: humiliate and devalue; that's his defining trait. He is the only genius; the rest of us are retards. He thinks the apartment belongs to him alone, but they gave it to all of us! He actually wanted to exchange it for a one-bedroom for our son, a studio for himself, and the dregs for me. How he screamed, that son of ours! I've got to get him to a psychiatrist, too. He claims my husband has signed all the papers, but that means nothing. I'll declare him legally insane and become his guardian! They want housing? He, and especially she, will get nothing!" Here Olga added a few invectives.

Suddenly Pulcheria blushed, but Olga didn't notice—she herself was purple in the face and kept on cursing and threatening, but all in vain.

"You should take Tsarina with you," Pulcheria calmly advised.

"Forget it," said Olga, deflated. "I'll go by

myself—it's not the first time." And with that she left Pulcheria alone.

Pulcheria, having passed Olga's exam, continued to sweat over her letters in her tiny windowless office. She worked in a great misery. It was almost March. She knew she had to wait patiently. One thing was certain: it wouldn't cost Olga anything to set Pulcheria's house on fire or to bribe the orderlies to get rid of him quietly. She also knew that he, her formerly mysterious guest, could have forgotten her already. Love likes secrecy and playfulness; it flees too much devotion and heavy emotional debt. It was possible that under the present circumstances he didn't care for love games anymore. It was even possible that he blamed ridiculous old Pulcheria for his troubles.

Pulcheria waited. The only change she accomplished was a quiet transfer to another division. Along the way she lost more weight, and almost fainted from weakness. It was the end of June when, coming home late from the library, she saw his gray suit and disheveled hair. Her guest stood up and opened the door. She stumbled shamefully. He supported her by the elbow and led her to the elevator.

A Happy Ending

Polina's life reached its final, happy phase when her aunt died and left Polina an inheritance. Polina had seen that aunt only once in her entire life, right before the end, when the doctor told Polina there was nothing she could do: the aunt was raving and didn't recognize anyone. Soon the hospital called to ask if Polina was planning to bury the body. Polina, who lived on a state pension, told the hospital she wasn't sure; she'd try to raise the money.

The next day Polina rose early and took a train to the small town where her aunt had lived. Naturally she wanted to look into whether her aunt had left an inheritance, for it was one thing not to have money for a funeral and quite another to let family possessions go to waste.

Polina didn't consider her aunt as family. As far as she was concerned, her only family was her son, but sometimes she didn't speak to even him for months. As for her husband, Semyon, Polina had hated him ever since his stay at a health resort years ago, after which he gave Polina gonorrhea and told everyone at the clinic that *she* had given it to *him*. Her only son had married and moved in with his wife; he did try to come back, but where was he going to stay? There were two rooms, and their son was pushing forty—he couldn't sleep with Papa or Mama, could he? Shame and tears—that was Polina's family life.

Polina loved only her grandson, Nikola, who visited them on holidays and occasionally stayed the night. He slept on a little folding bed and played chess with Grandpa and cards with Grandma. Polina adored her little angel until one day the entire family—the son, his fat wife, and the boy—moved in with her because of a burst pipe. The poor son returned to his flooded home to dry it out and paint and fix everything, while his family slept on camping beds borrowed from Polina's neighbors. One night Polina asked Nikola to bring her a glass of water to wash down a pill, and her angel asked indifferently, "What's wrong with your legs?" Polina didn't cry; no, she got up and walked to the kitchen on her poor, swollen feet while her grandson and his mama continued to watch a soap opera.

In time Polina began to think about ways to get away, to escape her circumstances, especially after her husband retired and stopped leaving the house. He lost the ability to converse in a normal voice and bellowed at her all day; in return Polina called him Clapper (her nickname for him since the gonorrhea episode), to which he responded with a string of obscenities, and so on. To an outsider their daily exchanges sounded like the blackest of comedies, but the spouses didn't laugh. After each screaming match they would crawl into their respective lairs, shaking with unspent tears, to pop heart pills; Polina would also call her college friend Marina to complain about Semyon and in exchange listen, bored to death, to Marina's complaints about her middle-aged daughter.

Polina—and this was her main problem—was tired of people. There was a time when she'd been capable of friendship; when she attended anniversaries and birthday parties, went swimming with her girlfriends, relished phone conversations about her friends' private lives. But all that ended when she became infected. She started to hate all gatherings, including family holidays, which she spent at the stove cooking while her son and his wife gobbled down all the food and then left to carouse with friends. She used to have hopes and dreams—to sew a new dress, to travel—but now she tossed and turned all night, captive to her thoughts, looking for but not finding a way out. She had heard of a mother who lost her child and then lay down in the snow, in an empty potato field, and fell asleep—they found her only in the spring. Should she do the same? By the time Polina got the call from the hospital, her last remaining love—for her only grandson—was essentially over.

When the call came, Polina considered what to do. She wanted to keep her plans secret from her husband, her son, and especially his wife, Alla, who would gladly poison both Polina and Semyon to get her hands on their apartment. On this subject the spouses understood each other perfectly—for the first time in ten years. One night at the dinner table, their son began mumbling about the advantages of a legal gift over a will "if something happens." "If *what* happens?" Semyon yelled back, and Polina echoed that it was beyond tactless to sit and wait for *that* to happen—look, your father's blood pressure is up; come, Senya, I'll check your pressure. With gentle care they checked each other's pressure, swallowed some pills, and retired to their respective rooms without saying good-bye to their son.

For a few days things were quiet in the house, but then their refrigerator broke down. Semyon accused Polina of leaving it open all night and refused to pay his share of the electric bill—things were back to normal.

Since the gonorrhea incident, this was Semyon's first major victory on the family front. Polina had always made more money than he did: she was an expert in military telephone equipment, while he (who had a PhD, by the way) lazed about in his underfunded research institute. After Semyon's STD, Polina began to eat separately, and Semyon, in his humiliation, would steal her food, saying, "So what did our hag cook for herself?" Still, if Polina was sick, then Semyon would drag himself to the pharmacy and even sweep the hall before the doctor's visit. He considered Polina's illnesses a result of her own folly; she should expose herself to cold, he lectured—a sick person must stay cold and hungry, like in a TB clinic! Polina had to crawl to the bathroom in a winter coat. She would call Marina, crying and swearing (while Semyon eavesdropped on the other line), and in return had to listen to the latest installment in the saga of Marina's daughter, who had picked up an illegal out-of-towner who didn't have a place to stay and who spent one night a week in the daughter's bed while Marina tried to sleep in her walk-through room (poor daughter, Polina thought). How could she reveal her secret to them—to Marina and Semyon?

And so she traveled to that faraway provincial town (an hour by train, an hour by bus, another hour by foot) all by herself. She found out the cost of a proper funeral and realized that even if she sold her earrings she couldn't afford to bury her aunt, who was going to be wrapped in plastic and thrown in some nameless hole. What could she do? Her son was again without work, Semyon was useless, and she herself would probably end up like Aunt Galya. She also found out that she could claim her aunt's apartment if she gathered the necessary papers.

On the train back Polina wept out loud. Her aunt's apartment was her only hope of escape. Also, this was the first time she was doing something just for herself; until now, everything she had done was for him, for Clapper—all the cooking, the cleaning, even her haircuts. She was a good-looking woman, but here she was, her charms wasted on one man, her only love, and he'd had to go and get a disease.

Back in Moscow, Polina flew around gathering paperwork, ignoring her husband's screams, which now sounded more like pleas—yes, Semyon suspected something. Two months later she lawfully entered Aunt Galya's apartment. She was met with the familiar smell of heart medicine and old clothes; saw peeling wallpaper and locked chiffoniers, which she easily pried open with a penknife. Inside she found pressed layers of ancient dresses that used to clothe generations of her family, all those women who had been buried in a coffin or without one, like poor Aunt Galya. For the past thirty years her aunt had lived alone in that squalid apartment without ever asking her, Polina, for assistance, although she had Polina's number and kept it in a visible spot on the wall. She also kept a shroud, slippers, and a cross—her funeral outfit—in a little bundle next to the bed; it was as though her aunt were asking her, Polina, for a last favor. Next to the bundle was a checkbook with some savings, to pay for the funeral, but the money was now worthless. Polina tossed the bundle with the other trash and kept only a family album and an ancient record player with some records wrapped in cloth sacks. Polina took these treasures home, thinking she'd impress her grateful family.

She arrived home late at night, and listened to Semyon's screams that he wasn't going to let a venereal slut use a shared bathroom; that first she must bring a note from the clinic, et cetera. Polina said nothing: she suddenly felt a surge of joy at the thought that soon she would escape this nightmare— that she had a way out. So that Semyon wouldn't lose his last marbles when she disappeared, Polina told him about an old aunt who was completely para-lyzed and whom Polina wanted to bring home, to Moscow, because the aunt's children refused to take care of her. On hearing this Semyon yelled that he refused to clean up after some old hag, spat at Polina's family pictures and records, and disappeared into his room—his dungeon, as Polina called it, where the window was always open and the lights didn't work.

The next Saturday Polina celebrated her birth-day. She cooked a meal, her trio of a family arrived, and after they stuffed themselves the shining Polina offered to play some old records and show family photographs (she slyly had added the best pictures of her young self to the album). She hoped that Nikola, the heir, would express an interest in family history, but he looked indifferently at the faded snapshots and shifted his attention to the TV to watch soccer. Polina's son and daughter-in-law again brought up the housing question: now they wanted Polina and Semyon to register Nikola as a resident of their apartment. "The fuck I will," yelled educated Semyon. "So that five years from now you could kick us both out? Ain't gonna happen! The Liapins," he continued, "registered their son at his grandmother's. The next day he announced he was going to have the place renovated, and he moved his grandmother to her sister's for three days; in the meantime he sold the apartment and left the country with the money!"

"And *we* know a certain babushka who lost her marbles and married some old idiot and registered him! Her daughter almost lost *her* mind! She'd been waiting for the old witch's apartment for decades!"

"Great idea, thanks," Semyon replied brightly. "I'll get married, too. Better than getting old with this venereal hag!"

"As you wish, but remember: I did your son a favor by registering him at my apartment, where nothing belongs to him, and now I'm getting punished for my kindness!" fat Alla concluded glumly, and went to get her coat.

They stomped out, forgetting the photographs. Polina cried a little over the dirty dishes and in the morning departed for her new home. At this point we could conclude our story, but life continued, and soon came the spring. Polina dug a tiny vegetable patch outside her new window and planted a few simple things like carrots and calendula. Every day she woke up and went to bed with a sense of quiet happiness. She tended her plants, walked to the village for goat milk, and gathered herbs in the fields, but after two months of this simple life she ran out of money and had to go to Moscow to collect her pension. She had forgotten the scandals, the constant humiliation, even Clapper—for good, she hoped. Nonetheless, after collecting her pension Polina forced herself to visit her former nest: she needed dry goods like flour and sugar, and also pickling jars. Without taking off her rubber boots she stomped into her old apartment and immediately saw Semyon sitting on her sofa in her room in filthy pajamas, smiling like a baby. His hair was completely white, he was unshaved, his chin was trembling, and the phone was lying disconnected on the floor. "Why is the phone disconnected?" Polina asked calmly. "I couldn't get through." Semyon nodded meekly and tried to fit the cord into the phone. His hands were shaking. Polina reconnected the phone, and immediately it rang; their son was calling from out of town, worried because his father hadn't answered the phone in three days. "I'll be back in a week!" the son said, and hung up.

Polina toured the apartment. In Semyon's dungeon she pulled off the stinking sheets and threw them into the tub; in the blackened kitchen she swept up the shards and trash and placed the dirty kettle on the stove. When Semyon, clean and shaved, was lying in a fresh bed and Polina was spoon-feeding him cereal, he stopped moving his toothless jaws, looked at her slowly, and whispered, "You must be hungry. Have a bite yourself."

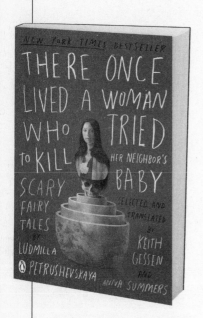

Fox Point Library - PCL